Sh[...] *herself be threatened . . .*

"The boy's missing. I've come to hear what you know about it."

"I?" Sarah stalled, offended by his rough manner and by his implication. What right had this man—this stranger—to accuse her! She was not about to tell him anything that might lead him to William. How could she know whether or not he meant the child harm?

His face was ablaze with an intensity that frightened her. His superb body was tense with the strength of the emotions that gripped him, and she was not in any way certain that it was safe to give him the information he demanded.

She lowered her gaze to where his hands hung at his sides. The beautiful, long fingers curled as if they longed to wring the truth from her . . . or as if they longed to wring her neck!

She gave herself a mental shake. To protect William, she must keep her wits about her . . .

Praise for Christina Cordaire's *Daring Illusion*:

"Fun!" — *Affaire de Coeur*

"Exciting!" — *Rendezvous*

"The bright, shining talent of Christina Cordaire gleams with added lustre in this deliciously original Regency romance."
— *Romantic Times*

Titles by Christina Cordaire

Beloved Stranger

Christina Cordaire

JOVE BOOKS, NEW YORK

BELOVED STRANGER

A Jove Book / published by arrangement with
the author

PRINTING HISTORY
Jove edition / February 1995

ISBN: 0-515-11550-9

A JOVE BOOK®
Jove Books are published by The Berkley Publishing Group,
200 Madison Avenue, New York, New York 10016.
JOVE and the "J" design are trademarks belonging
to Jove Publications, Inc.

PRINTED IN THE UNITED STATES OF AMERICA

10 9 8 7 6 5 4 3 2 1

Prologue

❧

ON THE LONG, WINDING DRIVE OF THE ESTATE, A TALL, hawk-featured man cantered along on a big black stallion. The dark figures seemed a part of the night that fell around them.

Arriving at the front entrance of the manor, they were met by a wiry little man in the livery of a groom. "Gor' blimey. What a 'oss, sir," the man burst out. "Looka that head, I ain't seen no finer!"

His words were an awkward combination of awe and knowledgeable praise. Then they trailed into silence as he took in the ominous figure before him.

The man smiled. The smile did nothing to reassure the groom.

"He's a handful." The man's voice was deep, the words rumbled. "Mind yourself."

Speaking to the great horse in Arabic, he handed Shiatan's reins to the groom and began stripping off his riding gloves as he mounted the steps to where the butler guarded the door.

That worthy took an involuntary step backward as the man approached.

The tall figure demanded, "Is Lord Branton at home?"

"I . . . I'll enquire, sir." The butler left the door

in the hands of a footman and fled to find his master.

The footman, no less intimidated than the butler by this unexpected guest, swung the door wider for the tall man to enter.

The unsmiling stranger removed his hat, threw his gloves into it, and handed it to the goggling footman.

The footman, awed by his presence, closed the door softly, as if afraid further to draw the man's attention to himself. Tiptoeing, he placed the hat carefully on a credenza beside the huge door, and tried not to cringe against the wall.

The tall, dark man locked his hands behind his back and fixed his hawklike gaze on the hall down which the butler had just scuttled.

He stood statue-still.

Waiting.

Almost immediately, John, Lord Branton came striding purposefully from the mouth of the hall.

Whatever Branton had been led to expect by the odd behavior of his butler, it was certainly not this.

Nothing could have prepared him for this.

He stood staring, dumbfounded.

His guest demanded in a voice charged with emotion. "Well, Jack?" His voice deepened. "Have I so greatly changed?"

Lord Branton clutched at the wall beside him for support. His mouth dropped open in a face that was rapidly draining of color.

In a strangled voice, he barely managed to utter, "My God!"

Chapter One

✑

HORRIFIED, SARAH WATCHED THE ACCIDENT HAPPEN. THE
bridge! The bridge was collapsing! The wooden
planks that formed the floor of the side of the
bridge nearest her were sliding from their sagging
support beam.

William! Dearest God! William and his pony were
about to fall into the rain-swollen waters!

She brought her whip down on her mare's rump
and sent her galloping toward the collapsing bridge.
Clods of damp earth flew from under Cymbeline's
flying hooves as they tore along the treacherous bank
of the stream.

Ducking branches that threatened to snatch her
hat from her head or her from the saddle, Sara cried
at the top of her lungs, "Hold on, William. I'm
coming!"

Fear rode the girl as hard as she rode her mare.
What if she were too late? What if the pony fell into
the flood and pinned its young master beneath it to
the stony streambed? What if the boy was swept
away, battered and broken against the rocks? Dreadful images of what might befall her young friend
filled her mind.

As if time on the bridge had slowed immeasurably, Sarah saw William's pony clawing like a cat at the tilting planks. Smooth, iron-shod hooves were no match for the steep angle of the timbers, however, and the two slid off into the roaring freshet.

"No!" Sarah's anguished cry rang through the glen and sent frightened birds flying from the trees. She clenched her teeth on the fear-filled words that rose in her throat and slammed her mare to a halt that brought a grunt of protest from the abused animal.

Without thought, Sara wrenched her mount around and sent her plunging into the water, driving her with whip and spur toward the spot where she'd last seen the boy and his pony. Cymbeline slipped and floundered on submerged rocks as Sarah pushed the mare forward with no thought of safety.

As the water deepened, the mare breasted it in erratic, bucking jumps that threatened to unseat her young mistress. Knowing full well that if she fell, her heavy velvet habit would surely drown her, Sarah pressed on, heedless in her determination. All that mattered was that she get to William.

In the foaming water, she saw the head of his pony, eyes wide and staring as it swam toward her. Even in his panic, Hercules was angling toward the bank. "Good boy! Come on, Hercules!" she shouted, encouraging the pony.

But William!

Where was William?

An inarticulate cry burst from her. Its wild anguish reverberated through the surrounding forest.

Frantically she looked around for help. Shocked, she saw that Jervase was still on the bridge! He sat staring at the broken portion of the bridge that had dropped crazily away and sent his young cousin plunging into the torrent. Why didn't he help? Why was he letting his horror hold him prisoner when he could be down along the stream's bank trying to reach William?

Jervase was riding Ajax. Ajax was twice as strong as Cymbeline. He could easily accomplish with his sheer bulk and greater brute strength what Cymbeline, who was fighting so hard to take Sarah to William's pony, attempted.

The gallant little mare was kicking up so much spray in her efforts, that Sarah didn't realize that the water she felt on her face was her own hot tears. "William," she moaned, "dearest, where are you?"

If only it could have been Hugh on the bridge instead of Jervase! Hugh, her beloved Hugh, would not have sat there like a statue. Hugh would have flung himself and his horse into the raging waters and rescued his younger brother before Sarah would have had time to utter her first shocked cry!

Suddenly, behind Hercules, above water only now and again, she saw William's strained face. Thank God! She was weak with relief. The child had grabbed his mount's tail, and was being towed along behind the struggling pony, sputtering and gasping for breath.

Sarah was momentarily relieved. Cymbeline felt her rider relax for that instant and stopped in confusion, tossing her head, her ears expressing her distress as they flashed first forward, then back. Sarah smoothed the mare's wet neck with one quick caress and tried to pull them both together.

Putting Cymbeline squarely across the path of

the pony, Sarah leaned down and caught up the smaller animal's reins. Then she fought to stay mounted as she turned Cymbeline toward the bank.

She was about to be dragged from her saddle by the weight of the struggling pony, when suddenly there was a mighty splash beside her. A startled whinny burst from Cymbeline. At the same moment, a strong arm shot round Sarah's waist, and she was pulled from her mare to the saddle bow of the man who had grabbed her. Cymbeline, left to her own devices, lunged to the bank and scrambled up and out of the torrent.

Jervase had finally come to his senses! Praise God! She sobbed her relief. But no! She could still see Jervase sitting his hunter on what was left of the bridge. Who, then?

A deep voice spoke in a language unintelligible to Sarah and the huge horse on which she now sat froze into immobility. The rushing water dashed against and foamed around its legs.

Sarah caught a glimpse of dark hair and a hawk-like face as the horse's rider flung himself out of the saddle behind her and into the stream. She saw him reach for William. As he touched him, the boy's head went under. "No!" she heard herself screech, terrified that the child would be lost.

The dark-haired man snapped a glance her way, his blue eyes full of anger. An instant later he had snatched William from the surging torrent, and was heading to the streambank with the boy safe in his arms.

The man's strength amazed her. The battering water, which would have swept Sarah away in an instant, could not divert him from his path by so much as a single step. He shoved the pony toward the bank, and lifted William out of the chilling water.

William still clung manfully to Hercules's tail, forcing the tall man to keep close to the pony as he headed back to the bank, William coughing and gagging in his arms. When he'd almost reached safety, the stranger spoke again to the great horse in the same melodious language Sarah had heard him use before.

The huge animal beneath her turned toward its master, and the swift power with which it moved nearly caused Sarah to slip off. One word, spoken sharply, and the huge animal's movement changed. Now it moved with smooth, careful precision to the bank.

Sarah relaxed the frantic clutch she'd taken on its mane, and sat erect, watching as Hercules lunged up the bank. Then the horse she sat on followed quietly, Sarah's sodden skirts dripping down its side.

Once over dry ground, Sarah slid down from the saddle. Even with her attention on William, she was conscious of the distance to the ground.

"Dearest, are you all right?" She struggled to the tall man's side, kicking the wet skirt of her habit out of her way.

William reached out for her, and she took him into her arms. His legs locked around her slight form to help her bear his weight. "Sarah!" His clutch on her neck tightened. She could barely heard his breathless voice. "Sarah," he whispered, "I was afraid."

Sarah squeezed him hard. "Of course you were, dearest. Anyone would have been." She raised her gaze from William to the man who had carried him from the stream.

Dark blue eyes returned her regard without expression. Again she was reminded of a bird of prey. The man's face was the most implacable she'd ever seen. He towered silently above her. He offered no words of comfort, no smile to belie her fears, no small gesture to reassure her. Sarah shuddered.

A twisted smile changed the man's face, but it merely rearranged his finely chiseled mouth. The smile never reached his eyes.

Determined to force her suddenly scattered wits to reassemble and do their duty, she said, "Thank you. You certainly saved William, and probably myself as well. I was not doing a very creditable job of rescue when you came along." She smiled at him, more to excuse her babble than to answer his travesty of a smile.

She waited expectantly for some sort of a reply. Instead, she saw the man flash a glance in the direction of the damaged bridge. He spoke sharply again in the foreign tongue, and when his horse rushed to his side, he leapt into the saddle and thundered away without a backward look.

"Well!" Sarah was indignant. She looked after him in utter amazement.

William pulled his head away from her neck and looked solemnly at her. "He wasn't very polite, was he?"

"Indeed he was not!" She erased the outrage

from her voice with an effort. "I wonder who he could be?"

"Yes." Jervase rode up and dismounted. "Just who was that chap? And what the devil did he mean, rushing off like that? He very nearly trampled you and William."

William reburied his face against Sarah's throat.

Sarah looked at her neighbor with a distinctly jaundiced eye. "I think," she said in her frostiest voice, "that I, for my part, shall just remember that he saved William's life while I only floundered around in the stream and——" She bit her tongue.

"While I simply sat on the bridge and did nothing. That's what you started to say, isn't it?" Jervase sounded peevish.

Sarah looked him straight in the eye.

"Yes, it is, isn't it? Blast it, Sarah, I was powerless to do anything. I was so shocked to see William's pony fall—the clumsy little beast—that I was rendered immobile."

William snatched himself upright in Sarah's embrace. She struggled not to drop him as he shouted at his cousin, "Hercules is not a clumsy little beast! He is not! He's a wonderful pony. Your old Ajax would have fallen just as fast . . . *faster* if the bridge had given way where he was standing!"

Jervase ignored the boy. "Oh, do put the child down, Sarah. He's far too heavy for a dainty little thing like you to hold."

Sarah opened her mouth to disagree, but before she could speak, William wiggled down and stood holding to her waist.

"Come," Jervase said impatiently, "both of you need to get home to a hot bath."

Sarah looked at him a moment. She still had not forgiven him for sitting on the bridge doing nothing. Finally she was able to say in a neutral tone, "You are quite right."

She fixed him with a look that was meant to convey more than she was about to say. "As soon as I have bathed and changed into a dry habit, I shall ride over to check on William."

"There is no need for you to do that, Sarah." Jervase was clearly displeased at her obvious distrust of his ability to take care of his young cousin and ward.

"Nevertheless," she said in her firmest tone, "I shall come for tea. William has had a terrible experience, and I shall not rest unless I have seen for myself that he is safely over it."

Jervase laughed mirthlessly. "I know better than to argue with you, my dear. We shall see you at tea. Mount up, William."

Sarah exploded with rage. "Is that all you are going to do? Just order the child to remount a drenching wet saddle?" Her eyes flashed dangerously. "The least you could do is put him up in front of you so that he could be a little warmed by your proximity. Or you could offer to wrap him in *your* dry coat."

William growled, "Don't want to ride with him."

"There. See. He doesn't want to ride with me." Sarah regarded Jervase stonily.

"Sarah, the child does not wish to ride with me." An expression of contempt filled her face.

Jervase began to struggle out of his riding coat. "Oh, very well. God, Sarah, you can certainly be a tyrant."

"Don't want his old coat," William managed between teeth that had begun to chatter.

Sarah bent to him quickly. "But you will wear it for me, won't you, dearest? I should be ever so worried if you took cold."

William looked mutinous a moment, then surrendered to her pleading smile. "All right. But only for you, Sarah."

Jervase snorted. At last, with a final effort, he was free of his exquisitely fitted coat. Impatiently he flung it around his ward.

"Mount up." He lifted William to his pony's back, ignoring the boy's squirming protest.

Sarah led Cymbeline to a fallen tree and mounted without Jervase's assistance while he was distracted by his young cousin. Somehow, just right now, she couldn't bear the thought of this man, her frequent dance partner at assemblies, touching her. She watched to see that Jervase was safely up, then turned Cymbeline toward home and gave her her head.

As she rode, she said a quick prayer for William's health. She could not bear it if the child should become ill. In addition to being a child alone in the world—except for Jervase, who could hardly be bothered—he was, oddly, her dearest friend.

She turned Cymbeline toward Fairlea, a hot bath and dry clothes. In her soaked habit, she was beginning to feel the coolness the earlier storm had brought to the afternoon.

Cymbeline was as eager to get home as she, and they flew along the grassy ride that cut through the woods to the road. Much of the way, Sarah, who was not a particularly religious young lady, found herself praying for the young Viscount's safety.

Chapter Two

SARAH WAS HALFWAY HOME, HER MIND LOST IN HER DEEP concern for William, when Cymbeline threw up her head and checked her pace. Another rider sat watching them approach.

"Oh, Jack. I did not see you." She smiled at her long-time friend, Lord Branton, both neighbor and their local magistrate.

"Obviously. Or you would not have all but ridden me down. What the devil are you doing soaking wet?"

Any other gentleman of Sarah's acquaintance would have apologized for his language—indeed, no other would have used it to her in the first place. Jack Branton, however, had known her parents well. He clearly felt that his having helped to raise her in their absence gave him the privilege of the plain speech he habitually used with her.

Quickly, Sarah told him of the accident at the bridge. He listened intently, and asked, "William is unhurt?"

"Yes, of course. Or I should never have left him. Jervase is taking him home, wrapped in his coat, to get him into a hot bath."

Sarah knew that Jack had been Hugh's good

friend. Because of that friendship, he had always kept an eye on his youngest neighbor, William Warren, Viscount Althurst, Hugh's baby brother. It comforted her to know he did so.

Jack turned his big roan gelding back in the direction of Fairlea. "A hot bath is just where you should be, young lady. Come along." With that he spurred his mount to a hand gallop and headed for the gates of Fairlea.

Sarah had no difficulty keeping the pace, and was grateful for the warmth the exercise brought her. It might be summer, but the storm that had swelled the stream to dangerous levels had left the weather unseasonably cool, and she was having trouble keeping her teeth from chattering.

When they arrived at the front steps of Sarah's ancestral home, Jack looked around for a groom. "What the hell is the meaning of this?" He scowled in the direction of the stables.

"It is nothing, Jack. Pray disregard it. It is just that this is the time when I usually return from my ride."

"What's that to do with anything?" Now he was scowling at her.

Sarah was so used to him she didn't even notice. "My cousins think I need to learn to use the kitchen door."

Before Jack could explode into the expletives she could clearly see were coming, Sarah added hastily, "It is a mere contest of wills. They think I need to humble myself a bit." Sarah shot him an impish glance as she slid, unaided, from her saddle. "I disagree."

Jack threw back his head and laughed. "I pity the

two of them if they hope to best *you* in such a contest. You've always been as stubborn as a goat."

"Merci du compliment, Monseigneur," she told him with some spirit. Then she smiled at him apologetically. "I should love to invite you in for tea, Jack—especially since it would thoroughly humiliate my cousins to learn that a guest had arrived without being attended by a groom—but I have invited myself to tea at Althurst so that I may see for myself that William has suffered no ill effects from his fall."

"Thanks for the thought but you'd have been wasting your time. Wouldn't accept an invitation that forced me to do the pretty to those two anyway, Sarah. Can't stand the jumped-up pair of them. Shame he is your father's heir under the entail. Monsters, your cousins, both of 'em."

Sarah merely smiled tightly up at him as she sent Cymbeline on to the stables. She, too, found it hard to bear the thought of Eustace taking her father's place.

Jack was still scowling, his fine, dark eyes full of distaste. "What happens when your horse arrives at the stables riderless?"

"Ah"—Sarah brightened—"now that is a sweet tale of pretty revenge, Jack." She grinned at him like an urchin. "Haley, my head groom, rushes up to the house with his boots as muddy as he can make them, and he and dear old Carsonby, our butler, you'll remember, rush into the drawing room in full cry, demanding to know whether to mount a search party to go and find my broken body.

"The uproar unfailingly distresses Cousin Letticia, who in turn sees to it that Cousin Eustace is blamed for it. Their peace is thus thoroughly cut up, and Eustace's digestion, according to him, ruined.

"As I say, it is petty revenge, but the three of us enjoy it monstrously."

Jack snorted. The abrupt sound spoke volumes. "Get inside and take that hot bath, Sarah."

Knowing she was well able to fend for herself, he turned his horse and cantered away without ceremony, leaving her standing on the steps.

Sarah shook her head, picked up her sodden skirts, and headed up the long stairs to where Carsonby, impatient to get her inside so he could join Haley in the game they played to discomfort the new master and his wife, held the door open for her.

She walked quickly to the grand staircase and hurried halfway up the first flight. There, she lingered to watch the fun.

She hadn't long to wait. Haley, the head groom, rushed in from the back hall, and flung himself against the double doors of the drawing room. Bursting through them, he shouted, "Miss Sarah's horse has come in without her!" His voice was loud enough to shatter crystal.

Carsonby, in his best butler manner, followed Haley, as usual, twisting his hands and adding to the din by crying, in his turn, "Miss Sarah's lost somewhere! We must go to her aid! Shall I turn out the footmen to search for her?"

Sarah could just catch a glimpse of Letticia, and saw her jump as she stabbed her finger. Her detested cousin's detestable wife was constantly doing needlework, and added her screech to the cacophony.

Eustace, far from sympathizing with his injured wife, instead bellowed, "You senile twits! You know very well that it is just Sarah insisting on entering by the front door! Again! Headstrong little brat refuses to be taught anything."

"Eustace!" Letticia took her pricked finger out of her mouth to chide him. "Not in front of the servants!"

"Get out! Just get out!" Eustace swung his arm violently in the direction of the door, his face as red as the hunt coat in the portrait of the late Earl over the fireplace.

Pulling his forelock, Haley stumbled backward toward the doors of the family drawing room. His uncoordinated movements left even more mud than usual on the Oriental rugs.

Carsonby backed out with a look of such horror at the new master's undisciplined behavior that he seemed not to notice when his elbow caught and toppled to its doom a vase from a small table near his path of retreat. Bowing awkwardly, his expression distraught, he pulled the doors closed behind him and Haley.

Once out of the drawing room, the two men straightened, grinned at each other, and struck their palms together in a firm handshake to commemorate another job well done. As one they cocked an ear in the direction of the quarrel in full bloom inside the room they had just left, and departed, each to his own duties, replete with smug satisfaction.

From her place on the stairs, Sarah watched them go, smiling. Then she turned and hurried up the rest of the stairs. Winifred, her maid, was waiting at the door of her room, a severe expression on her face. "Grinning like that at your poor cousins' discomfort. I don't know what has got into ye lately, Sarah Constance Fotheringay. Ye're a regular imp of Satan betimes."

Given no time to answer her abigail's charge, Sarah was hauled into her room and stripped of her damp habit. Then she was helped into her waiting bath by her faithful Winifred.

With a sigh she sank into its welcome warmth. Trust Winnie, in spite of her scolding, to have an eye to Sarah's welfare.

Cousin Letticia had expressly forbidden that hot water be carried to Sarah's room for her bath, so every day Winnie had the footmen bring the huge cans of water first thing in the morning, and put one into each corner of the fireplace. By the time Sarah came in from her ride and wanted her bath, the water in them was hot enough to warm the next two tall cans Winifred had the footmen lug up from belowstairs.

The one time that Letticia had stopped the footmen to check the temperature of Sarah's bathwater, she had been happy to find it as cold as she intended it to be.

Sarah had been goaded by Letticia's obvious satisfaction to extol the joys and invigorating properties of a cold bath.

Letticia, taken in by Sarah's seemingly fervent praises for the benefits of a cold bath, was unable to resist trying one for herself. Far from seeing her sallow complexion bloom into the cream and rose one Sarah swore came from her habit of taking cold baths, Letticia found her own skin tinted slightly blue.

Thinking back on that episode, Sarah felt a little guilty. She also felt more than glad that her birthday, the arrival of which would free her from the company of her odious cousins, was only weeks away.

Winnie scrubbed Sarah's back vigorously. "What happened to ye, that ye come in all soaked and your second-best habit well nigh ruined?"

Sarah told her, and Winnie was so concerned that Sarah might have been swept away by the rain-swollen waters that Sarah sought to divert her by telling her of the scene she had witnessed in the drawing room. Winnie tired to look sternly reproachful, as her Scots Presbyterian upbringing dictated, but soon both dissolved into laughter.

When the laughter died, Sarah gave herself to the pleasure of being fussed over. Sitting quietly in the comforting warmth of the tub and her abigail's care, she thought back over the events of the day.

She suddenly realized it was decidedly odd that Jack, who was, after all, the district magistrate, had asked no questions about the strange dark man who had saved William and her. How very unlike him that seemed to her. Jack was usually the most careful of men.

She would have been considerably reassured if she had known that Jack was even now instructing three of his grooms to keep a watch over William.

"Thank you, Grimsby." Sarah smiled at the Althurst butler.

Grimsby had always made her welcome. He had

been doing it since her childhood, and she counted him as a friend. "Where is William, Grimsby?"

Grimsby corrected her gently. "*His Lordship* is in the north drawing room, having tea with his guardian, Your Ladyship."

He was quite used to her finding her way about the house, as she had run tame there most of her life. Now, however, since Mister Jervase had arrived, things were a little different. Jervase was next in line for the title, and had had himself appointed guardian to his young cousin. The servants found him rather high in the instep. As a consequence, Grimsby escorted Sarah to the north drawing room.

"Lady Sarah Fotheringay, Your Lordship," he announced.

"Sarah!" William slipped down from his chair and ran to greet her.

"That will be all, Grimsby," Jervase snapped as he watched the butler linger to smile fondly at the two friends.

Grimsby made no move to leave. After all, Jervase was not master here.

Sarah saw Jervase scowl and whispered hastily to William.

"Another cup, please Grimsby." William's youthful voice galvanized the old gentleman, and with a murmured "Very good, Your Lordship," he left, closing the doors carefully behind him.

"Cheeky!" Jervase all but exploded.

"Not at all, Jervase." Sarah regarded him levelly. "Grimsby is quite proper. It is you who are out of line. It is not your place to dismiss William's butler from his presence."

Jervase flushed deeply. "You are right, of course."

Sarah was of the opinion that he'd barely managed to get the sentence out civilly. It didn't matter to her, however. Just so long as he remembered that it was William, and not he, who was Viscount Althurst.

The rest of the afternoon passed pleasantly enough with Jervase paying pretty compliments, and Sarah ignoring them to play jackstraws with William on the hearth rug until it was time for her to go home to dress for dinner.

Chapter Three

SARAH WAS STILL TRYING TO THINK OF SOMETHING TO TAKE William's mind off his shocking accident the next morning as she sat with her feet tucked up under her and watched as Winifred came stealthily into the library.

"There was no letter from Aunt Penelope." Sarah sighed, disappointment evident in her voice.

"How did ye know?" Winifred regarded her indignantly. "I haven't told ye yet."

Sarah refrained from telling Winifred that her face had given the game away. Instead she got right to the problem. "This isn't at all like Penelope. She has always been most prompt in answering my letters. Her correspondence is very important to her now that she is so much out of society."

"Aye, that she is, the poor lady. 'Twas a sad thing for her husband to have treated her so."

Sarah gave Winifred a repressive look. "Sad? Shabby, rather, for him to put period to his own existence and leave dear Penny to face his creditors all alone." She frowned. "I suppose when Papa died, there was simply no one else who would pay his debts."

Sighing heavily again, she ran her fingers through

her short, dark curls. "I think life is grossly unfair sometimes, Winnie. If I had been in a position to help, Uncle Harry might still be alive."

"No doubt!" Winifred's disapproval of Sarah's late uncle was evident in her tone of voice. "And still gambling away every farthing he got his hands on too! A handsome rogue was your uncle Harry, Miss Sarah, but the bane of your dear father's existence. He would have been so to ye as well."

"Well, all that doesn't help my aunt. Somehow I feel that the money I raised by selling Mother's ring must be depleted, and Penelope is too proud to let me know that she is below the hatches. I must go to London and see why she has not responded to my proposition."

"Please do not use cant phrases," Winifred corrected her former nursery charge from force of habit. " 'Below hatches,' indeed!" she muttered before returning to the point. "And just how will ye do that when ye know full well that your cousin will never give you permission to take one of the coaches? No, nor any of the men."

"I shall have to ask William, I suppose."

"Little Lord William?"

"Yes, and it might just serve to take his mind off his accident. He has coaches enough, and I know you'll approve my trying to avoid using my own and upsetting my cousins."

"Hrummph." Winifred scowled at her mistress. "They aren't your own until your nineteenth birthday, Sarah Constance. Hiding from your cousins the fact that the coaches and horses will all be yours come August is what ye intend, more like."

"Well, yes, there is that." Sarah smiled at her

sweetly. "I suppose it's true that I have no desire to spoil the surprise I have for them on my birthday."

"Surprise, indeed. Shock is more what I call it. Shame on ye, Miss Sarah. The Lord himself would scold ye for the delight ye're taking at the thought of marching out of here and leaving your cousins afoot on the day ye inherit."

"I seriously doubt that, Winnie. The Lord has a sharply honed sense of justice, dear friend." She cocked her head, thinking a minute. "That's probably why we are constantly asking Him to have mercy in the Morning Service. Few of us want justice."

She left off her musings before they sent her abigail into a sermon and told her briskly, "Now help me change and I'll go ask William to help."

Cymbeline, fresh and full of energy, made short work of the ride to Althurst. Sarah apologized to William's head groom. "I'm sorry to bring her to you so hot, Heatherstone, but I *must* talk to William, and she simply would not walk the last mile quietly for I couldn't spare time enough to ride her down."

Heatherstone smiled at her. "You just go along to Lord William, Lady Sarah. I'll have Jim cool her out." His voice took on a note of disapproval. "We get quite a few hot horses now that Mr. Jervase has come."

Sarah tucked away the fact that, in the barn, Jervase wasn't well thought of as she ran up the stairs and into the house. So much for yet another suitor.

Sarah despaired of ever finding a man with whom she could bear to spend the rest of her days.

She certainly had no intention of permitting someone to take over and rule her life who was not well
thought of by the servants!

"Good morning, Grimsby." She smiled at the
butler, who had anticipated her knock and was
holding the door wide. "Where is William?"

Grimsby broke one of his own cardinal rules and
smiled indulgently. "Lord William is in the morning
room, I believe, Your Ladyship." He took her gloves
and riding crop and waited while she removed her
long-veiled beaver from her dusky curls and handed
it to him. He looked after her fondly when she dashed
off to find William.

A cool voice spoke at his shoulder. "You'd think
someone would have taught her to move like a
lady."

Turning, Grimsby looked at the new housekeeper
with obvious distaste. He hated the way she sneaked
up on people, and he had no intention of tolerating
her comment about Lady Sarah. "Lady Sarah *is* a
lady, Mrs. Nethers. Therefore she may move in any
fashion she pleases and it will be that she moves like
a lady."

He stared down his nose at her. "It is left to others
to move well by aping their betters."

Ignoring her shocked gasp, he turned his back on
her. Congratulating himself on an intentional insult
well delivered, he placed Lady Sarah's riding hat
on the table beside her whip and gloves as if he
were handling the Crown of England and permitted himself another smile.

He was glad Lady Sarah Constance came to visit
the young Viscount frequently. So, indeed, were all

the staff at Althurst. All except the witch who had just stomped away in a huff.

As if that would bother him—newly come interloper that he and the rest of the Althurst servants found her. The staff had bonded together against her.

They had even less liking for her bull of a brother. Grimsby had lost no time assigning him to the stables after he had seen how the brute behaved with the maids.

His thoughts returned to Lady Sarah. He sent up a terse prayer of thanksgiving. Without her, there would be very little happiness in the young Viscount's life.

He wished he didn't feel that things had gotten worse since the arrival of Mr. Jervase. There was no way around it, though; they had.

The fragile happiness the servants had been able to build for their young master had been shattered by the acerbic presence of his cousin and guardian, Jervase Warren. Now there was only Lady Sarah.

Moving off to go about his business, he wondered when there was ever going to be peace at Althurst again. The servant's hall guessed that it would be ten long years before the young master would have enough age on him to get rid of his cousin Jervase, though a few said that Lady Sarah would surely help him to do it sooner.

They were all settled in to wait, however long it took, for they were as devoted to the boy Lord as they'd been to his sweet-natured older brother.

Remembrance of the Sixth Viscount caused Grimsby to stop halfway across the great hall and cast his glance upward to where the portrait of his former master hung above the archway through which Lady Sarah had just passed. The tall, fair-skinned, well-fleshed young man in the painting looked back at him with the eyes of a dreamer.

Grimsby stood beneath the portrait and wished for the thousandth time that they could *know* what had become of the young Lord. His disappearance almost nine years ago had thrown all their lives into chaos.

Grimsby remembered it well. It had been three months after the young heir's twenty-third birthday. He had gone to buy a christening present for the child his dear mother was expecting—the present Viscount.

He'd never been heard of again.

No one could credit it when he failed to return. The Fifth Viscount, his father, had led the exhausting search for him until it had broken his own health and he had succumbed to an inflammation of the lungs.

The shock of losing both her husband and her son had been blamed for the loss of the mother when she took to childbed prematurely. The missing Hugh Warren had become the Sixth Viscount, even while the search for him continued.

It had been a sad, sad time for them all. What had been the happiest of families had been destroyed.

And the gloom lingered still at Althurst.

Little Master William had become the Seventh Viscount Althurst when his brother had been declared dead almost on William's seventh birthday, poor tyke. Grimsby heaved a sigh.

There had been yet another heartbreaking day when they had held burial services for Lord Hugh.

That day had put an end to the hopes they had all had that the Sixth Viscount, Hugh Warren, might someday be found. Grimsby shook his head sadly.

For a long time, Grimsby had thought that matters couldn't have been worse. By pulling together, however, the household and Lady Sarah had begun to piece together a happy life for the little Viscount. Like the rest of the staff at Althurst, he would always be grateful for the deeply caring Lady Sarah.

Then six months ago, the child's cousin, Jervase Warren, with his beautiful "housekeeper," Mrs. Nethers, in tow, had come with papers declaring him Viscount William's guardian.

Things had not been the same since. With a sigh that shook his tall frame, Grimsby returned to his duties.

Sarah, throwing open the door to the morning room, found William sitting in a chair next to a window fondling his spaniel's ears with an expression of such sad boredom that it tore at her heart. The joy that lit his face at the sight of her brought an answering smile to her own. "Hello, William!"

William hugged her fiercely. "I am *so* glad you have come, Sarah."

She glanced around the beautifully appointed room as she returned his hug. "Good!" she whispered as she embraced him. "Jervase isn't here."

His fat spaniel stood at her young master's heels languidly wagging her stub of a tail in greeting. The wagging went through every inch of her plump little body.

Sarah stooped to pet the old dog. Fluff was the

only one left of the three spaniels that had used to trail around after Hugh, the late Viscount.

Sarah had known Hugh Warren, Sixth Viscount Althurst, as she'd grown up at Fairlea. In spite of his being years older and away at school much of the time, she had many fond memories of him.

She particularly remembered his kindness through that terrible first year after her mother and father had been killed in the fire that had swept the guest wing during the Kingsleys' house party. Hugh had been unfailingly kind to the diminutive, shattered nine-year-old Sarah, and there was no way she would ever forget him. He had become the standard against which she measured every man she met. And always they came up short.

Like everyone else who had known him, Sarah longed to learn what had happened to Hugh Warren. With them she had grieved at Hugh's memorial service almost two years ago when he had finally been declared dead after his long absence.

Abruptly she rose from petting the dog, flinging away unhappy memories with a toss of her curls. "William," she began briskly. "I have come to ask a boon."

"Oh, Lady Sarah!" The child's eyes were shining. He was happy and eager to play knight to Sarah's lady in distress. It was a game Sarah had invented for his amusement. "A boon. What will it be?"

"My fair Knight, I must enlist your aid—and your company—on an adventure."

"Oh, I say, Sarah. What is it that I may do to be of service to you?" His gaze was intent. He longed to do for Sarah.

Sarah's face became serious. "I want to go to

London to see what is the matter that Aunt Penelope hasn't answered my letter."

William thought a moment. "Would that be the letter you had me frank for you last month?" His obvious pleasure at being able to perform such a service at so young an age was evident. England was not exactly full to overflowing of nine-year-old lords. "But isn't this a bit early?"

"Not for Aunt Penelope." Sarah bit her full lower lip worriedly, then said, "She always answers me within two weeks. She *always* has. So something must have befallen her, and there is only me to care."

"There's your cousin Eustace. He's the head of your family now. He should see to this matter." William looked at her sternly, his eyes too large and too serious in his soft, child's face. "He shouldn't let this fall on your shoulders, Sarah."

Sarah shook her head, and her curls danced. "Whether or not he should, I can assure you he has. He says he has no interest in my aunt's plight." She scowled at William. "Says she's the concern of her own family, can you credit it?"

"I shouldn't think that a gentleman would behave in just that way." William strove to weigh his words. "Grimsby and my tutor both tell me that I must care for the welfare of each and every member of my house and household." His brow furrowed. "Sometimes that seems awfully hard. But if *I* must do it, then surely Eustace should too, I think." William's eyes were full of concern.

"Oh, William." Sarah grabbed him and hugged him quickly again. "Whatever would I do without you?" She pushed him out to arm's length and gazed at him solemnly. "You really are so wise. Far beyond your years, my friend."

The boy blushed with pleasure. "Thank you." Squirming out of her hands, he said with some embarrassment, "I suspect that comes from having grown up with absolutely no one my own age. My friends have always been adults, you know." He smiled at her mischievously. "In fact *you* are the youngest of them!"

Sarah chuckled at him. She gave him another quick hug and moved toward the chairs in front of the fireplace.

William grew serious. "You still haven't told me what you want me to do." He tagged after her, the spaniel following to settle with him on the hearth rug.

"It is really quite a lot to ask, dear." She let him think about that, as she shoved a cat out of the chair she wanted, then went on. "I want you to see me safely to and from London to check on my aunt Penelope. I want you to be my escort, if you please, kind sir."

The cat hissed at the spaniel as she passed her. William said, "Be good, Bathsheba," with very little hope that the bad-tempered tabby would obey. Then he got back to what interested him.

"A trip to London." For a moment the thought threatened to overwhelm him. Then he squared his small shoulders. "You mean for me to order one of my coaches to take you there?"

He was careful not to let Sarah see that he had misgivings. "And I am to escort you," he said wonderingly. Then, more firmly, "We shall have to take your abigail, for that is only proper." He cocked his head, thinking. "And perhaps we shall have to wait until next week, when Jervase goes to the Daltons' house party."

"Yes, of course. That's a splendid idea." She beamed at him. "How very practical you are! Eustace and Letticia are going to the Daltons' too, so that would be perfect. It would be hard for either one of us to get away with our watchdogs hanging about."

"Very well. When should you like to go?" He tried hard not to sound hesitant. He would rather die than disappoint Sarah, but he really was out of his depth. He looked at her earnestly. "I don't know a great deal about traveling, you know." He blushed, embarrassed. "I've never done any," he informed her solemnly.

"I'm sure you will do very well, William. I'll find out from Haley how long it will take to get to Town." A thought struck her. "Perhaps we should take him as well. He's familiar with London, and that might come in handy."

"That's a capital idea, Sarah."

She returned his smile as she warmed to the subject. "Things might go better if you order the horses and coach at the very last minute so that no one will think to stop us, don't you agree?" Her eyes lit with enthusiasm for their conspiracy. "You can pretend that you just want to play at traveling. Grimsby will humor you, he always does . . ."

"Then we must leave him a note, of course."

"Of course."

"Yes." He frowned in concentration. "Also, mightn't it be a good idea if Haley were to come here to drive me to get you?" He looked up at her sheepishly. "Just in case they won't obey me at the stables, you know."

William sighed heavily and looked at Sarah wistfully. "You're the only grown-up who thinks I'm worthy to be treated as an equal, you know."

Sarah made a face at him. "Pray don't complain to me, of all people. You may be young and thus have a problem in that way, but it is something *you* will outgrow. I, on the other hand, shall *always* have it." Her voice took on a tinge of bitterness, "for I am a woman, and no man thinks *us* worthy to be treated as an equal."

"Oh, Sarah, surely that is not true in your case?"

"Don't I wish *that* were so!"

"Well," he said, stoutly loyal, "I think you are every bit as smart as Jervase."

"Huh!" Sarah said inelegantly. "So is Fluff." She threw out a hand to indicate the lazy spaniel.

William forbore to comment.

Sarah jumped up and held out her hand, ready to dash off. "Come, let's go choose which coach we will take, shall we?"

Fluff had lifted her gray-muzzled head in response to her name, and looked toward them as they chatted. Now she wagged her tail, scrambled to her feet, and trotted after them, delighted to have someplace to go.

The noises and smells of the city threatened to overwhelm them. After the quiet and space of the country, the streets of London were teeming with life. Horses neighed, drivers shouted, and hawkers called their wares. The din was fearful.

Carriages crowded carriages between drays and

carts. People on horseback threaded their way through the perilous traffic. Less fortunate people on foot took their very lives in their hands to cross the busy thoroughfare.

Sarah and William stared out at the passing scene and held on to one another's hands as to a lifeline. Sarah's eyes were only a little less wide than the boy's, and she doubly regretted the cold that had kept her from asking her sneezing abigail to accompany her.

"Oh, Sarah. I am so glad you suggested we bring Haley."

"Why, William?" She asked only to distract him. She herself took comfort from Haley's presence on the box.

"Because London is so big! We'd never find your aunt Penelope if you didn't have someone who knows it."

Suddenly, Fluff, content until now to doze in her basket, lifted her head, looked around in confusion, and began to bark hysterically. While Sarah and William stared at her in astonishment, the little spaniel leapt up on the seat next to Sarah and flung herself toward the window.

Hanging on to the sill with her forepaws, she jumped frantically at the opening. Sarah grabbed her. "Fluff! Be still, you'll fall out!" Sarah held tight to the dog, and looked out to see if she could discover what had so upset the dear old thing.

In the press of traffic, she saw a huge black horse not ten feet from the carriage. Thinking she recognized the splendid beast, she strained to see the rider.

Just then a dray pulled up beside them, forcing

the rider away before she could be sure, but she was almost certain that he was the dark, hawk-faced man who had appeared at the stream when William had had his accident.

"William! Look!"

William shoved over to see out her window. "At what, Sarah? What is it you wish me to see?"

"Oh, do be quiet, Fluff." Sarah set the squirming dog down in her basket on the floor.

Fluff looked once more toward the open window, whined fitfully, and finally lay down. Her big brown eyes watched the opening without blinking.

"William, look around. I think I saw the big black stallion and the tall stranger that hauled us out of the stream!"

William obligingly craned out the window. "I don't see him, Sarah."

Over his head, Sarah searched the crowd. "No, I don't either now." She frowned. "Strange, I did think I saw him." She turned a serious face to William. "Did you notice? It was as if Fluff sensed something, wasn't it?"

"Do you think she was trying to warn us?" William's eyes were like saucers.

"Warn us?" Sarah settled back against the squabs with a thoughtful expression. "Oh, dear." Sometimes animals did sense things.

She cast her mind back to the brief moments she had spent in the company of the tall, dark stranger. He *had* gotten them all out of the water safely, she had to give him full credit for that. But there had been that awful moment when he had reached for William and . . . had he *shoved* William's head under as he grasped him?

She remembered that she had screamed, and the stranger had shot her a look of hot anger. Had her scream and consequent close attention kept him from some terrible, dark purpose?

Oh, dearest God! Had the tall, dark man been trying to see to it that William drowned? Her blood ran cold at the thought.

And had Fluff, old and half dead as she was, sensed some further peril from the man a moment ago when he had been close to the carriage? Had she been trying to warn them?

She bent down and scooped the little brown and white dog up into her arms. Holding her in her lap, she reached an arm out to gather William to her side.

Suddenly she was terribly, terribly cold. Suddenly the day had taken on an ominous feeling that strongly oppressed her.

She desperately needed this close contact with her young friend and the reassuring warmth from the dog's furry little body.

Chapter Four

SARAH FORGOT ALL ABOUT THE MYSTERIOUS DARK STRANGER when they arrived at her aunt and late uncle's town house to find the knocker off the door. "Oh, William, look." She sounded desolate.

"Don't be sad, Sarah." William patted her hand. "We shall find her, truly we shall." He called out, and the two footmen he had ordered to accompany them—the only two who would obey him—went to the houses on either side of Penelope's to make inquiries.

Returning to the coach, the one called Ned told Sarah, "They don't know where she went, Your Ladyship. But they was kind enough to tell me that your aunt was great friends with the widow on the corner, and that if anybody knows where she's got to it would be the Widow Kent." He bowed himself away from the carriage, flushed with pride in the effort he'd just made on the little lady's behalf.

"Thank you, Ned," William said gravely.

"Oh, yes, thank you," Sarah echoed, then called out to the driver, her own head stableman. "Haley, please take us to the corner, to the Kent house."

"Do you want to get down yourself, Sarah?" William offered tentatively. "I think it would be best."

"As usual, you are as right as rain, William," Sarah told him briskly and rewarded him with a smile. "I am sure Mrs. Kent will only tell us where to find Aunt Penelope if we introduce ourselves properly."

". . . and dear Penelope had no choice, you see. No choice at all. Harry's creditors were demanding that the house be sold literally out from under her! Yes, out from under her." Mrs. Kent wiped at her eyes with a tiny scrap of lace-trimmed linen and sniffed loudly. "My poor Penelope. Why wouldn't she consent to move in here with me? I have so very much more than I can ever, ever use both in room and in the world's riches. And I do miss her so! Most dreadfully."

Sarah gazed solemnly at the lachrymose lady. Since she had absolutely no idea what reasons her aunt may have had for refusing the widow's hospitality, there was nothing she could say. She refused to offer consoling platitudes that purported to express her aunt's opinions when she had no hint of what those opinions might be.

Instead she offered her own thoughts as consolation. "Aunt Penelope is indeed fortunate to have a neighbor like you, Mrs. Kent. While I can have no idea why she refused to move in with so generous a friend, not being privy to her thoughts, I can only suspect it was her pride that kept her from doing so." Her smile was winsome. "We are, alas, a prideful family, you know."

"Prideful. Yes, yes. She was a very proud lady. Such a proud lady."

Sarah tried not to be annoyed by Mrs. Kent's use

of the past tense in regard to Penelope. "We really should be going to find her, Mrs. Kent. The sooner I locate my aunt the sooner I can send word back to you that she is safe."

William, as always, understood her mood, and simply took Sarah's hand and held it. As they passed through narrow and even more narrow streets, he held tighter—as much to reassure himself as to bolster Sarah's flagging spirits.

"Oh, William." She looked at him with enormous eyes as the traveling coach stopped.

Haley called down, "I'll be unable to get the coach out of here if I go any farther, Lady Sarah."

The houses in this part of London leaned precariously toward one another over the roof of the coach, and the open drains in the center of the cobblestoned street filled the air with noxious smells.

William dragged out his handkerchief and pressed it over his nose. Wide-eyed, he waited for Sarah to make the next decision.

Ned assisted her to alight, and she saw for the first time the unsavory men who loitered nearby. She held her head high and pretended not to notice their obvious interest in her party as she told Haley, "Please have the coach turned around by the time we come back, Haley."

By the grunt with which her old retainer replied, she knew what he thought of that endeavor. Looking at the narrow alleys at whose crossroads the carriage stood, she didn't envy him his task.

The footman came running with the news that he had discovered the number they sought, and Sarah and William, hands tightly clasped, followed him to the door of the ugly little house that was her aunt's new address.

At Ned's knock, a rough female voice called, "Whadaya want?"

Sarah's fear for Penelope galvanized her. "I want my aunt! Open the door this instant!"

To her surprise, the door flew inward, and she saw a tall woman in the dress of an upper-class servant. The maid dropped her a curtsy, and said in her normal voice, "Forgive my rough words, Your Ladyship. I speak that way for our protection. Rough speech is safer here."

"Of course," Sarah said absently, but she had eyes only for the lovely woman standing behind the giantess. "Aunt Penelope!"

Penelope rushed to embrace her niece. "Dearest Sarah! How relieved I am to see you."

Sarah hugged her as if she would never let go.

Finally Penelope gasped, "Sarah, you must introduce your escort," and disentangled herself.

Surreptitiously wiping at her eyes, Sarah presented William, delighted that her dear Penny had not treated him like the child he appeared.

"We are most relieved to find you safe, Lady Penelope," William assured her in a high, sweet voice. He bowed gravely over her hand.

Penelope smiled. Captivated by this cavalier in miniature, she breathed, "Thank you, Your Lordship."

Her husky little voice enchanted William. He shot a look at Sarah to let her know he approved of her aunt.

The three of them stood beaming at one another

for a moment. Then Penelope said, "This is Maude. I could not exist here without my faithful Maude, so you must know her."

William bowed. "Maude."

Sarah said gravely, "For taking care of my aunt, I thank you most sincerely, Maude."

Maude's severe expression gave way to a broad smile. With the smile she changed into a rather attractive woman and relaxed visibly. "Thank the Lord that you are come, Lady Sarah. Lady Penelope is so stubborn that she'd not allow me to send for you, but she stands in sore need of rescue. There are rough men about who are without the manners to which you are accustomed, Lady Sarah, you may be sure."

"We must get my aunt away immediately."

Maude heaved a gusty sigh. "Thank Heaven!"

Penelope's throaty laughter interrupted them. "Very well, you two. Sarah"—she threw her arms wide—"I am ready to be rescued. Take me, I am yours."

"With the greatest pleasure!" Sarah moved to embrace her aunt once more. They shed a few tears, then pushed away from one another and laughed happily.

"I really was only trying to stand on my own two feet, you know."

Sarah tried not to scold. "But dearest, this is no place for you. Why did you come here?"

Penelope had the grace to blush. "The wine merchant needed to be paid, then the butcher said he had sick children, and the candlemaker . . ."

Maude took a long stride forward in the middle of their conversation. "They all tore at her like vultures, Your Ladyship. And poor tenderhearted thing that she is, she soon gave them all that money you sent for her to live on until your birthday."

Sarah was in instant sympathy with Maude's feelings. "Indeed, I don't blame you for being put out, Maude. I thank you again for the care I see you've taken of her." She patted the abigail's broad hand. "I think it would be best if you packed her right now."

She looked around the shabby room. "I can see you brought only a few pieces of furniture." She indicated a dainty lady's desk, the chair that belonged to it, one very fine mirror and a tambour frame. The rest of the few things in the room were obviously not her aunt's. "I think Ned can find a way to carry them with us on the roof of the coach. If there is anything more, we shall engage a carter to bring them to Fairlea."

Maude said, "There's only the linens, her clothes and such. Two trunksful is all she brought away from Belgrave Square, milady. The trunks will fit on the coach too." She cast a sour glance around the humble room. "I'll have it all packed in twenty minutes.

"Forgive me if I don't offer to brew you tea, Your Ladyship, but it won't do to have your fine coach linger in this neighborhood."

As if giving weight to her warning, Fluff started frantically barking, seemingly right outside. Maude took the sound as an admonition to hurry, turned and rushed up the narrow stairs to the floor above, determined to begin her packing.

William ran to the door. When he opened it they

saw that Haley had managed to back the traveling coach down the lane to just beside the door.

A group of ragged men surrounded the coach. Sarah heard one of them say, "Ifen ya wants out of 'ere with yer coach in one piece, ye'll pay." He bounced a sturdy bludgeon against the palm of his hand.

White-faced with anger, Haley shouted at him, "Away with you, or I'll call the watch."

There was a shout of raucous laughter. "Lissen ta' im! 'E don' even know the watch don't dare ta' come in 'ere."

Ned and the second footman rushed out of the house to reinforce Haley, who ordered them to take up positions at the heads of the horses.

William turned and whispered to an angry Sarah, "I should have thought to arm my footmen."

Ignoring the fact that the sun was almost set, Sarah said, "One shouldn't have to go armed in one's capital city in broad daylight!" She surged past William. "Here! You men. Go away this instant. You can't bully honest travelers. This is England, after all."

William came to stand protectively at her side.

The gang of ruffians turned toward her in astonishment. It took a moment for them to regain their senses. Then the man with the bludgeon advanced on Sarah. "What be that bauble ye're wearing, milady?"

"Ned! Run for the watch!" Sarah shoved William back behind her and grasped the edge of the door to slam it shut, but the man jumped forward and grabbed hold of it before she could do so.

"Now, now, me pretty. Like I jus' tol' your coachman, the watch don't come 'ereabouts."

Sarah folded her fingers around the gold locket that had been her mother's, hating the way the man looked at it. She stared back at him haughtily, but she was afraid to speak for fear her voice would tremble.

"The watch knows better, missy. The watch don' come back 'ere."

"No," said a cool voice from the other side of the alley. Heads whipped around to find its owner. "But I do."

Sarah's gaze shot toward the speaker. It was the rider from that day at the bridge! Mounted on his huge midnight stallion, he sat easily, the barrel of a pistol laid casually in the crook of his arm. It was pointing straight at the man who held on to the door. Eyes implacable, he challenged the ruffian.

The man let go the door as if it were on fire.

"I think you have business elsewhere, have you not?" The words were casually spoken, but the man at the door had no difficulty hearing the underlying threat. Without a sound he turned from the door and scuttled away. He and his companions vanished into the shadows of the alley as if they had never been.

Sarah watched the point at which they had faded into the gloom incredulously for a long moment then turned to express her gratitude to the man on the black stallion. He was gone!

She frowned mightily. "Blast!" She slammed the door so hard it shook the whole flimsy wall in which it was set.

"Sarah!" William stared at her reproachfully.

She had the grace to look sheepish. "I know. I shouldn't say that."

"Well, I was actually reproving you for nearly bringing our defenses down." His eyes were alight with amusement as he indicated the trembling wall.

"Oh, William, what a brave little soldier you are!"

"Thank you, Sarah. It is ever so nice of you to say so. I am not, however, so brave that I want to be here when those men return." Grave blue eyes regarded her from his youthful face. "So do you think you and Lady Penelope could possibly help Maude to pack?"

Chapter Five

"WHO WAS *HE*?" PENELOPE CLASPED SARAH'S ARM WITH both hands and gave it a little shake. "You must tell me who our handsome rescuer is, dearest."

"I would, gladly, Aunt Pen, except that I haven't the foggiest notion of his identity, myself."

"Oh, how perfectly charming." Penelope stood smiling fatuously in the direction of the door. "An unknown champion."

Sarah stared at her aunt.

Penelope smiled back, unruffled. "So tall, so handsome! He has eyes like a hawk. So piercing, so . . . so almost . . . fiery." She hugged herself. "And those shoulders. So wide! It must take three men to get him into his coat." She positively twinkled at her niece. "Did you see the way he sat his horse?"

Sarah wanted to stamp her foot. "Aunt Penelope! You are behaving in a most shocking fashion and I wish you would desist." She frowned at the willowy beauty she had thought, until this very instant, would be a most proper chaperon.

She was relieved, and indeed almost disbelieving, to see her aunt instantly return to normal. She was dismayed, however, to hear her say, "Really,

Sarah. You must not chide me for admiring—as we ladies of the *ton* do—the man who has made it possible for us to leave here safely."

That distracted Sarah from the scold she was about to deliver, and instead she said with a sigh, "Indeed, you are quite correct in that. It was admirable of him to help us." Then she added as if she could not help herself, "Though it did not seem to be much of an effort on his part. He has but to glare and men quake."

"Sarah." Penelope's eyes lit with interest. "You are being uncharitable. It is so unlike you!" She sounded as if she had made a delightful discovery.

Sarah felt a strong urge to change the subject. She herself could not understand why the tall, swarthy man caused her to react so unpleasantly. She was certainly not desirous, however, of having her aunt pry into her feelings. "Uncharitable or not, I say we should make the best of the time he has bought us, for I've no doubt that those ruffians will return as soon as they feel safe enough to do so."

"Oh, dear, yes." Penelope looked around the dingy little room. "Maude, are we packed?"

Sarah was glad to see she had successfully distracted her aunt. She breathed a soft sigh and tried not to wonder what it was about the stranger on the black horse that disturbed her so.

"Yes, milady." Maude crossed the room from the bottom of the stairs with two portmanteaux and walked calmly to the coach. Ned placed them in the luggage compartment at the back of the vehicle, then he and the other footman wrestled the two trunks to the roof and secured them there.

Haley kept watch as if he expected either the

ruffians or the mysterious stranger to reappear. From the expression on his face, Sarah couldn't tell which filled him with the most apprehension.

Hastily, the men loaded the few possessions Penelope had managed to save for herself from her husband's creditors. Lashing them to the roof with the trunks, they covered the whole with a tarpaulin against the chance of inclement weather.

When they had finished, Ned, who'd been constantly looking over his shoulder for the ruffians, held wide the door to the ugly little house. With all his might, he willed the three women to hurry out to the waiting coach, where the young Viscount stood politely holding that door for them.

Everyone heaved a sigh of relief as they settled themselves in the vehicle. None of them could hold back their relieved laughter to hear that collective evidence of their relief. When they had caught their breaths, William rapped over his head on the roof and called out in his sweet soprano, "Take us home, please, Mr. Haley."

"With the greatest will in the world, Your Lordship!" Haley answered fervently and began to drive carefully out of the warrenlike area.

Soon he had them on a proper thoroughfare, and minutes later on the pike that led toward home. When the iron-tired wheels of the coach left the cobblestones of the London streets and ran onto the dirt surface of the highway, William ordered, "Spring 'em, Haley!"

A cheer went up from their little band as Haley did just that.

*   *   *

As they rocked along at a gentler pace to rest the horses after their first rush away from the city, William snuggled against Sarah. She looked down at his tired face, and smoothed his hair back from his forehead. "Thank you, my gallant Knight."

William fought a yawn to say, "We did it, didn't we, Sarah?"

Sarah smiled at him tenderly. "You did it, William."

Across the coach, Penelope smiled from beside her tall maid. "Yes, Your Lordship. And Maude and I shall be forever grateful for your timely rescue."

Sarah felt William swell with pride.

"I am delighted to have been of assistance, Lady Penelope." Another yawn ruined the effect of his grave courtesy, but no one minded. "Pardon," he murmured, his hand half rising to cover his mouth, only to drop back into his lap as he tumbled into sleep.

Sarah cradled him gently against her side and patted him soothingly. The Seventh Viscount Althurst slept in the arms of his friend.

Sarah and Penelope exchanged smiles, then Penelope settled into her corner and closed her eyes.

Maude shrugged herself firmly into her own corner, smiled at Sarah, and permitted the tension she had lived under while she had protected her mistress to drain from her. Within minutes, she dozed.

Sarah was still too excited by the events of the day to follow their good example. Left to her own devices, she thought of the first moment she had seen the man her aunt called their "unknown champion."

Vividly, the turbulent stream and William's struggling pony returned to her mind's eye. Again she saw the tall form plow through the water to the boy's pony.

In cruel clarity she saw again how William's head had been thrust under when the stranger reached him.

Even in the calm of retrospect she was unable to decide whether or not the dark man had deliberately pushed William under. The thought filled her with terror.

He was so strong. The rush of water that had nearly been her undoing had failed even to stagger the man. Surely a man of such physical power could have done just as he liked with a small boy caught in the turbulent waters. What chance would a small child have had against him?

If she had not been there, would he have . . . ? The thought was too dreadful to pursue.

And too preposterous, she told herself. Surely the man would not have rescued them today if he had had foul designs on William. Surely he had been a hero that day at the bridge. But the insidious doubt crept back into her mind: if he had been helping, why run away as he had?

She felt a little shiver pass over the back of her neck. She couldn't help it. Deep in her heart, on a level she could not quite reach with her reasoning mind, she sensed that there was something about the stranger that threw her innermost being into turmoil.

Obviously, something was very much amiss.

William was too precious to her to put him at risk. Of necessity she would watch over him closely until she could come to a conclusion about the man on the midnight stallion.

She must decide. Was he indeed a champion? Or did he represent a real and potent threat to the well-being of her young friend?

It was deep night by the time they reached their village. They passed through it at a walk, resting the weary horses as well as making themselves less noticeable.

When they arrived at Fairlea, every light was out.

Sarah said, "Can you manage with just your portmanteaux, Pen?"

Penelope assented with a nod, and Sarah asked Ned to carry the bags as far as the French door to the library that she had carefully left unlocked what seemed an age ago.

Maude said, "I can manage from here," and took them from the footman.

Ned looked up at her and nodded, never doubting her ability to do so.

Sarah instructed him in a whisper, "Ride back inside the coach and keep His Lordship from falling off the seat, please."

Ned nodded again and was gone. An instant later they heard the coach move off.

Sarah sighed with relief. Haley would drop Pen's things off at the stable, drive William, his footmen, and his traveling coach home and return on the horse he'd ridden over to Althurst. Sarah's part would be to sneak Penelope and her maid into her room.

That there would possibly be repercussions tomorrow did not in the least concern her for the moment. Just right now, all she wanted, and she suspected all the other two wanted as well, was to get safely upstairs to their beds, lie down and go to sleep.

Straightening her shoulders, she led the way across the library, out into the hall that led to the grand staircase, and up the steps and along the hall to her room.

Quietly she opened the door. Even as tired as she was, she stopped to smile at the sight that greeted them.

Her bed was turned down on both sides, ready for her and her aunt; a snug pallet had been made up for Maude under the windows; and on the table in the center of the room, there was a cold collation with enough food to feed a small army.

The good fairy who had performed these mercies sat covered by a light blanket in the chair before the fireplace, her feet on the footstool and her chin on her chest. Every now and again as the three travelers prepared for sleep, moving very carefully so as not to disturb their benefactress, a tiny snore escaped her.

Sarah went and tucked the blanket carefully around her. She stood a moment, gazing fondly down at her abigail.

She had no doubt that the scold she would receive from Winifred in the morning would cause the other repercussions she was expecting to fade in comparison. While Winnie was generally a forgiving person, Sarah knew that she would not be easily pardoned for arriving home in the dead of night and not waking her to tell her she was safe.

She stood quietly beside her faithful maid, torn

between the gratitude she felt that someone in her cherished home still cared about her and the forlorn feeling she always got when she allowed herself to think about her missing family.

After a moment she added a log to the fire. Knowing her despondent mood was merely the product of her bone-deep weariness, she pushed her self-pity aside and went across the spacious bedchamber to join her aunt in her familiar bed.

Here in the comfort of her own room, she could rest at last. To that end, she resolutely put aside her speculations about the mysterious stranger who had rescued them.

Almost immediately, she slept. But her dreams were full of the austere face of their rescuer.

Chapter Six

IN THE MORNING, SARAH SLIPPED OUT OF HER BED BEFORE all the others awoke. Moving with the stealth of a thief, she dressed in her oldest riding habit and stole quietly from the room.

Ghosting down the stairs, she let herself out the back door and headed for the stables. Today she was going to attend to something that had been bothering her since William's accident.

Today she was going to try to find out *why* the bridge had collapsed. It seemed strange to her that a bridge that was looked over carefully by her late father's groundsmen, and probably William's as well, several times a year, should collapse, and so suddenly. Now, with the urgency she had felt about her aunt assuaged, the bridge had become the most important thing on her mind.

The water had been too swift and too deep for her to chance it before now, but it had not rained the past two days. She hoped she would be able to manage. She intended to try.

"Thank you, John," she told the sleepy groom who had saddled Cymbeline for her.

"When will ye be coming back, milady?" Even half asleep, he followed Haley's standing orders always to keep Sarah's schedule in mind.

"I shall not be above an hour." She smiled at him, glad to see how they looked after her. She found it rather sad that such a simple kindness could so move her, and wondered if it was the same for William.

He, too, was an orphan, and he, too, was in the hands of relatives—or in his case, only one—who seemed to care nothing for him. Someday she must see if he grieved over it as she was afraid the very observation she had just made indicated that she did.

With a heavy sigh, she put the matter out of her mind for now and left the stableyard at as close to a walk as she could persuade her fiery little mare to do. Once away from the manor, she gave Cymbeline her head and tried to work her down a bit before she turned her toward the stream that marked the boundary between Fairlea and Althurst.

When she arrived at the bridge, she tied her horse and walked to the brink of the stream where what was left of the structure still met and was anchored deeply into the bank. No one had repaired the damage to the side that had been destroyed, but the debris seemed to have been removed—or perhaps had been swept away by the water. At least, there was none about that Sarah could see.

The bridge remained undamaged on its upstream side, so Sarah walked across on that part to the end nearest Althurst. It was at that end that the downstream side of the bridge had collapsed and spilled William and his pony into the water. There, she jumped lightly to the bank, and attempted to peer under the bridge.

"Oh, dear." She could see nothing by leaning as

far out from the bank as her hold on a slender oak sapling would permit.

"Drat." She let go the oak and bent to catch up the train of her riding skirt.

She cast a doubtful look at her tethered mare. "Pray I don't drown myself, Cymbeline," she told the curious animal, and turned to pick her way down the slippery bank to the water.

Without warning, she lurched forward then nearly toppled backward as her booted foot slipped on the mossy bank. Sliding wildly, she tried to save herself by clutching at a low-hanging branch. The tips of her fingers touched it. With an effort, she barely caught the branch. Now she was tottering inches from the swiftly moving water.

"What the hell do you think you are doing?" The rough masculine voice rose in volume as its owner neared her precarious position.

Startled, Sarah jerked her head up. With that, she lost every vestige of balance and pitched toward the water.

"Damn and blast!" He was beside her in one jump. His strong arms encircled her to catch and sweep her up to safety. He held her easily in the cradle of his arms as the water swirled around his booted legs.

Sarah looked up into the face that had haunted her dreams and struggled to regain the breath that her sudden contact with his hard body had knocked out of her. "You!"

He scowled down at her. "Just what the blazes did you think you were doing?"

"I was—"

"And what would have happened to you if I

hadn't been here?" he demanded fiercely. "Didn't you come close enough to drowning the last time you were here?" His eyes shot blue sparks.

Sarah saw the harsh lines around his mouth and a part of her wondered why she wasn't frightened. Here she was, alone in the woods with the man she suspected of having caused the accident she came to investigate, and she was casually resting in his arms.

That last thought galvanized her to action. She could hardly continue to permit this man to hold her thus. It was a shocking breech of modesty!

"Please put me down."

"I'll put you down if you will promise to stay on the bank." His eyes were stern.

"I cannot achieve my purpose from the bank, sir." Her own eyes were determined.

"And that is?"

Sarah felt the words rumble in his chest where she rested against it. "Sir, this is quite improper. I must insist that you put me down."

She knew she should be struggling to get free of his embrace instead of trying to identify the spicy smell of his cologne, but such a sense of innate power radiated from him that she was not about to try.

As if he sensed her conflicting emotions, the tall man bent and placed her carefully on her feet at the edge of the stream. He did not, however, let her go, but grasped her arms just above the elbow.

Sarah felt it wise to accept this—at least until she stood on firmer ground. She was framing a demand when he anticipated her.

"If you were coming to look under the bridge to

see why the boards gave way and dumped . . ."—
Sarah was sure she heard a slight hesitation—"His
Lordship and his pony, then I can tell you that the
support beam had been sawn through."

Sarah gasped. "But that would constitute an
attack on William!"

He looked at her piercingly. "You must be more
objective. There is also the possibility that it may
have been a work of random mischief." He watched
her face closely, his eyes slightly narrowed. "Perhaps it was to catch the next person over the bridge,
no matter who it might have been."

"Yes," she agreed, "that could be true." She
looked at him steadily. She couldn't miss the intent
wariness of his gaze. She wondered how he would
react if she confided her fear—no, her intuitive
certainty—that the damage to the bridge was meant
to injure William.

Preoccupation with her thoughts made her care-
less of her next statement. "But we have never had
anything like this occur before." The minute the
words were out, her eyes widened. She realized
that what she had said could be taken to imply that
this stranger was to blame.

Her fears were justified.

His eyes darkened to the blue of storm clouds.
Through clenched teeth he asked, "You are saying
that nothing like this happened before I came, are
you not?" His eyes burned at her and his voice was
harsh with accusation.

Bravely she met his gaze. "I am sorry to say so,
but yes, that is the truth." She braced herself for his
reaction.

She could hear his teeth grind as he demanded,

"And just why are you sorry, little Sarah? Because you don't wish to offend an innocent man, or because you fear me, alone in the woods as we are here?"

While her stomach might knot with apprehension, Sarah realized with wonder that she was certain, deep inside, that she had nothing to fear from this formidable man who somehow knew her name.

"I do not understand it, precisely, but I am not afraid of you."

For a moment he was startled by her frankness. Then, a smile of such poignant beauty changed his face so greatly that Sarah was amazed. It altered and softened his harsh countenance. He was years younger than she had thought him, she realized. And rather handsome, too. She stared.

"Thank you, Lady Sarah," he said, his voice deeper, holding a warmth she had not heard there before. "Your woman's heart has not played you false. You, of all people, have nothing to fear from me."

He stepped up on the bank then, slipped an arm around her, and helped her up the moss-grown slant back to Cymbeline. Lifting her lightly to her saddle, he handed her her reins. "Have a care. Someone sawed that timber, I assure you."

She watched his lean visage as he spoke, strangely touched for the second time that day. She saw a ragged white scar that disappeared into his hairline at his left temple, and in the back of her mind she wondered how he had gotten it.

He was looking at her earnestly. She felt she was seeing the true man for the first time. She studied his face so intently she almost failed to hear his next words.

"Sarah, have you thought that if you had been coming back from Althurst, it would probably have been you and this mare that fell into the stream?"

Startled, she could find no answer for him.

"Take care," he said again. He turned Cymbeline toward home and clapped her lightly on the rump.

Outraged, the dainty mare sprang forward into a gallop, leaving the stranger standing there at the bridge.

Back at the house, Haley met her at the front steps. His face was full of wry humor. "I was ordered to meet you, Lady Sarah." He took hold of the mare's bridle. "I am to tell you you're wanted in the south drawing room immediately."

Sarah, certain that she knew why she was thus summoned, dismounted as if she had all the time in the world. It had been so long since she had been attended while she dismounted at Fairlea's front door that she was determined to enjoy it to the full. "Thank you, Haley," she said with some formality. Then, in a whisper, "Is it very bad?"

Haley chuckled. "Carsonby says your Aunt Penelope seems to be unruffled, milady." He grinned. "Unfortunately, her presence seems to be upsetting your cousins."

Sarah looked about her as she gathered her skirts to begin her ascent, "Isn't it a lovely day, Haley?"

He stroked Cymbeline's neck, waiting to take her to the stables until Sarah dismissed him. "Aye, that it is, Your Ladyship."

With a gracious nod, Sarah calmly walked up the

broad stairs to where Carsonby waited with the door held wide. If she put out of her mind the evident unpleasantness before her, it was almost as if she were back at the Fairlea she had always loved. Surely Aunt Pen would not blame her for savoring it for just a brief moment.

The south drawing room was full of sunlight, but that was the only illusion of warmth. Long Sarah's favorite room among the formal chambers at Fairlea, today it was less than welcoming.

It seemed to be arranged in warring camps. Though there were only three people in the room, Sarah could almost hear the sounds of battle as if armies clashed in the chilly emotional atmosphere of the drawing room.

Penelope stood at one side of the room. Clad in a lovely yellow muslin gown of becoming simplicity, she not only looked like a shaft of sunlight, but also decidedly cast the other female in the room into the shade.

Letticia wore a pomona-green morning dress that did nothing for her sallow complexion. Her thunderous expression did nothing for her features.

As Sarah entered the room, Penelope was saying pleasantly, "Of course, I realize my unannounced presence in your house this morning must come as something of a surprise, Letticia, but I could hardly arouse the innkeeper when I arrived in the middle of the night."

"I am certain I cannot see why," Letticia snapped. "Innkeepers are quite used to being awakened by travelers." Her lips were a thin line.

"Ah, but you see, Lettie, I was so weary I had no energy with which to concoct an excuse for needing the comfort of his establishment when the house of my husband's family was so near." She turned and looked earnestly at Eustace. "And, of course, I was loathe to so embarrass you."

While Letticia sputtered, Eustace caught Penelope's meaning exactly. He coughed to gain time to order his thoughts into a pattern that would not show him for the uncaring man that he was. "Yes, of course. You did precisely the right thing to come to us." He cleared his throat to stall for the time to phrase his next words. "Ahem." He decided to bluster. "I do wonder, however, just how you gained entry."

Immediately understanding that her aunt was keeping her own adventure to London a secret, Sarah moved smoothly into the breech. "I heard the coach." That was certainly true. She had heard it most of the preceding day.

It was obvious to Sarah that Penelope had misled Eustace into thinking she had come alone, and equally obvious that no one had noticed—or at least had not reported—her own day-long absence. She decided not to clear up these misconceptions.

Eustace turned on her. "Ah, so *you* let her in."

Sarah corrected sweetly, "Yes, I let *Lady Penelope* and her maid in. There was no need to disturb the household. I was able to make them comfortable in my chamber."

From her place by the window, Penelope cooed, "And we rested very well, dearest. Thank you." She turned her limpid gaze on Eustace. "Now we have only to devise a tale for the innkeeper with which you will be happy, dear Cousin Eustace, and my maid and I will be on our way." Giving Eustace a moment to digest that, she turned to Sarah and said in pretty supplication, "You will be my frequent visitor during my stay, will you not, my dear?"

Eustace quickly grasped the danger to his social reputation. "No, no," he blurted out. "It would look decidedly odd for you to reside at a common inn while you are in our neighborhood. You must remain here as our guest."

A sound like steam escaping from a kettle burst forth from Letticia.

Eustace quelled her with a glance. "I'm sure my wife," he said in deadly tones, "can make you more comfortable than you were last night sharing a bed with Sarah." He glared at his spouse. "Can you not, Letticia?"

Letticia pursed her lips to disappearance. Grudgingly she admitted that she could. Adding "I'll see to it immediately," she stomped from the room.

Penelope glided to her niece's side. Slipping an arm around her, she steered her to the door. "Thank you, Eustace," she said in her low, throaty voice. "I am certain that I shall very much enjoy the time I spend here with you. Fairlea has always been justly famous for its hospitality."

Eustace stood dumbfounded. He couldn't decide whether or not he had just been insulted.

Sarah turned admiring eyes to her aunt. She wondered if *she* would ever be able so deftly to handle Eustace and his detestable wife.

Somehow she thought not.

Chapter Seven

THINGS WERE STILL FAR FROM COMFORTABLE AT DINNER that evening. They had all tacitly agreed to behave as if all were well, however.

"There is an assembly tomorrow night. I suppose you shall both want to go." Letticia spoke coolly from her place at the long table in the handsome formal dining room for which Fairlea was renowned. From her tone of voice, neither Sarah nor Penelope could fail to discern her complete lack of interest in their wishes.

Sarah looked at her in surprise. Somehow she had thought Letticia would not show her lack of consideration in front of a relative stranger. In her surprise, she said hotly, "You have certainly waited late enough to tell us about it."

Letticia opened her mouth to flash back at her.

"Ahem, ahem." Eustace began clearing his throat while he sought the words to reprimand his young cousin.

It was Penelope's voice, however, that slipped smoothly into the uncomfortable moment. "Ah," she said. "How delightful. I have never been to a country ball. Do tell me how one dresses for these affairs, Letticia."

Sarah subsided. She was thoroughly sick, though, of the way she always had to learn of the assemblies through Jervase or some other neighbor because her cousin, to whom, of course, invitations for the family were quite properly addressed, was too mean-spirited to inform her.

Suddenly, she was overwhelmed by a strong desire for her birthday to come so that she could move to her own establishment and be done with all the pettiness with which she was constantly treated here. As much as she loved and would miss Fairlea, she could hardly bear to stay beneath its roof with her cousins a moment longer.

She became aware that Penelope was still speaking. ". . . and of course in all the bother of settling me, an unexpected visitor, anyone would have forgotten to tell us of the assembly. There is no harm done. We shall have all day tomorrow to prepare."

Again Sarah admired her aunt's tact, this time a little grudgingly. Then she gasped at her next statement.

"I cannot think why you did not receive my letter telling you to let me know if my visit would be inconvenient."

What a prevarication! Sarah was shocked. When Penelope turned her limpid gaze her way and asked solicitously, "Do you need a pat on the back, dear?" Sarah could only stare.

The next night was cool and clear, and, for a miracle, everybody was ready to go before Eustace had time to get impatient. They even settled themselves in the carriage without anyone getting upset.

The ride to the assembly hall was pleasant enough,

with Penelope deftly turning aside any darts Letticia sent Sarah's way. She was even able subtly to change Eustace's sour comments into pleasant remarks. In fact, she did so with such consummate mastery that Eustace was beginning to think he had gained some skill at playing the gallant. His face wore an unaccustomed smile as they rolled into the village.

Under the light lap robe that kept any dust from their gowns, Pen squeezed Sarah's hand. Sarah squeezed back and they held hands all the way to their destination.

On their arrival, such a swirl of people pressed forward to greet Sarah that her cousins were jostled aside. Eustace's smile disappeared and he and Letticia entered the ballroom in a huff.

The loss of their company disturbed no one.

Sarah's friends clamored good-naturedly to be introduced to her aunt. Sarah had promised them, in notes written that very morning, that they would "simply adore" her, and they were eager to ascertain that for themselves.

Penelope, in an India muslin gown the color of the peridot necklace for which it had been designed—a necklace that had been sold just after her husband's demise more than a year ago, to satisfy some of his debts—looked like a queen. Her light Titian hair, piled on her head like a crown, heightened the effect.

Sarah watched Penelope charm the crowd around her. She was as proud of her aunt as she could be, and stood smiling to see the way her friends accepted her. She noticed that Pen glanced toward the tall, dark stranger where he stood with her neighbor, Jack Branton, but had hardly had time to wonder about it before a voice called her name, and she turned to find Jervase at her elbow.

"You look like the cat who swallowed the canary," he said. "Why?"

"Oh, hello, Jervase," she said with little enthusiasm. Then in a brighter tone, "How is William?"

Jervase looked annoyed. "William is fine."

"To answer your question, I am pleased that my friends are glad to meet my aunt."

"Oh, yes. She is to be your chaperon when you set up your own place, isn't she?" He looked toward Penelope with more interest.

"My companion, Jervase," Sarah corrected him. "I am too old to need a chaperon."

"You'll only be nineteen, Sarah."

She hated the way he seemed to try to belittle her maturity of mind. Sarah knew herself to be as steady as most matrons. Steadier than many, she thought as she watched giggling Mrs. Frampton and gushing Lady Feldmere.

She was determined, however, to give him a soft answer in spite of her feelings and said, "Many young ladies are married and have started their family by that age, I would remind you."

Jervase looked at her then in a manner Sarah could only decide was speculative. She felt a faint hint of annoyance.

Surely he couldn't still be thinking he might try to attach her—and her considerable fortune, she thought wryly. She had hoped she had made it clear that they would not suit when he had hinted at an alliance last August on her birthday.

She shook out her fan and used it in an agitated manner. *Heaven forbid* that she marry a man like

Jervase Warren. After all, his stablemen did not admire him.

An instant later, she forgot to be annoyed with him as she again followed her aunt's glance across the room to where the dark stranger stood beside Jack. She would get Jervase to take her to them! At last, here in a civilized situation, she was going to meet the man about whom she was so curious.

Properly introduced, she would have a far better chance of inquiring into his reason for being in the village of Little Fairview. That would certainly help her to discover the man's intentions.

It annoyed her no end that without an introduction, a young lady was terribly hampered. Especially if she were bent on an investigation of any kind. She had already flown in the face of propriety by speaking to the stranger at all.

"Look, Jervase." She slipped her hand through his arm. "There is Lord Branton. I have not seen him this age. Will you please take me to him?"

Jervase frowned down at her. "He was here at the last assembly." His expression left no doubt that he understood to whom it was she wished to be taken.

"But I didn't get to speak with him." She regarded him steadily, trying not to frown at him.

Sensing she would leave him standing and take herself where she wanted to go if he waited longer, he said resignedly, "Very well, Sarah," and crossed the room to the two men.

The stranger watched them come. He had never seen Sarah dressed to advantage before and the sight nearly took his breath away.

She seemed to float toward him in a light silk gown of the same emerald-green as her eyes. Her short, dark curls were carefully brushed into artful disarray, and a ribbon that exactly matched her gown was threaded through them. The jewellike green heightened her color, and her rosy lips and cheeks contrasted markedly with her pale, clear skin.

The winsome child had, all unconsciously, grown herself up to be a great beauty. He felt a strange tightness in his chest.

Sternly reminding himself that he was here on grim business, he ruthlessly stifled his admiration of the Lady Sarah Constance Fotheringay.

"Sarah." Jack acknowledged her. Turning his head, he greeted her escort without enthusiasm. "Jervase."

Sarah smiled at her old friend radiantly. "I am so glad to see you, Jack."

Branton was unimpressed by her smile. It was clear Sarah was up to something. "Permit me to introduce my friend." He indicated the somber man at his side. "Lady Sarah, may I present . . . Hassan Triste. Hassan, Lady Sarah Fotheringay and Mr. Jervase Warren."

The man called Hassan bowed over her hand, and Sarah felt a pleasant tingle run upward from her fingers where he lightly clasped them.

Taking her hand back gently, she watched him bow coldly to her companion. The gesture seemed oddly in keeping with the man.

If she were forced to choose but one word to describe Hassan Triste, she thought with an inward sigh, it might have to be "cold." "Austere" and "forbidding" jostled "mysterious" for a moment in her mind, but when he looked at Jervase, the word that won was "cold."

But she remembered that moment at the edge of the stream when, with one heart-wrenching smile, he had seemed completely to change. And for just that one moment he had seemed so . . . so familiar.

She wondered about his name. While he was certainly sun-burnished to a darkness foreign to that of an Englishman, she had the feeling that he was not from one of the Arab countries as his name suggested. In fact, oddly, she was certain in her heart that he was one of their own.

"Sarah, where have you gone?" Jack was scowling at her.

"Oh." She blushed and offered as excuse the first thing that popped into her mind. "I was just thinking that 'Triste' was the French word for 'sad.'" She turned wide green eyes toward the man who called himself Hassan. "Is that not so?"

"It is so," he replied in a grave voice that, in league with his intent gaze, wrapped the two of them in a world of their own.

After a breathless moment, Sarah blinked and took a deep breath to restore her wits. She had no intention of mooning like a nodcock in the middle of the Little Fairview Assembly Hall.

Jack came to her aid, asking in a dry voice, "Sarah, may I have this dance?"

She looked at him a little vaguely, then smiled and gave him her hand. From that dance to the end of the evening, she was never without a partner.

Never once would she let herself admit that her enjoyment of the ball was in any way impaired by the fact that Mr. Triste did not dance with her.

*   *   *

The assembly over, and all their good-byes said, the party from Fairlea entered their coach. Penelope settled back against the maroon velvet squabs with a soft sigh. "My, what a pleasant diversion that was."

Letticia snorted. "Surely," she said in an aggravated tone, "you cannot mean that it compares in any way with balls you have attended in Town."

Penelope answered honestly, "Not for grandeur, of course. Nor for brilliant company. But I think the conversation was lively enough, the people ever so much more obliging, and I think"—she cocked her head thoughtfully—"that I would say I distinctly preferred it to many of the superheated crushes that are balls in London."

She could not help noticing the avid way in which Letticia hung on her every word. Suddenly, Penelope could not help herself.

Knowing full well that a good Christian would never succumb to the temptation to deliberately bait another human being, Pen made a mental note to ask forgiveness later. "Of course, Letticia, you would be more than able to make these comparisons for yourself, if only you had brought Sarah out this past Season."

Letticia absorbed the blow and turned an accusing face to her spouse. "There, Eustace, you see? You wretched miser. Just see! You have denied me the pleasures of Town with your pinchpenny ways." Her eyes shot fire at her husband. "If you had not resolved to save the money it would cost to give Sarah a Season, *I* might have enjoyed the delights of

London. *I would have gone to balls in London!*" Her last words were a wail.

Eustace scowled, and proceeded to fill the lamplit coach with "Ahems."

Sarah, appalled at Letticia's outburst, tried for the hundredth time not to mind that this ungracious pair were taking the places of her beloved, charming, *well-bred* parents. She stared out the window at the moonlit countryside.

Penelope, instantly contrite that her twitting of the sour Letticia had discomforted Sarah, said, "I found your friends delightful, dear."

Sarah pulled her attention back into the carriage. "I am so glad. You can see why I have no wish to relocate."

"Indeed, I can. Easily." She let a quiet moment and her feeling of contrition pass, then probed. "I found Hassan Triste especially fascinating."

She kept a close eye on her niece's face as she said that. She was not surprised by the quick blush she saw there, and smiled softly.

Finally, she mused with satisfaction. A gentleman who had caught Sarah's interest. It was about time.

When her niece made no comment, however, Penelope put her head back and closed her eyes.

In the privacy of her thoughts, she remembered the way Sarah's eyes had strayed frequently to where Mr. Hassan Triste had stood all evening, and decided that she must find out quickly if this "Hassan" was a suitable person for her precious niece to be so attracted to.

When she had thought about that for a moment, she gave serious attention to her own behavior. Casting her mind back over the events of the evening, she wondered if anyone might have noticed how often her own eyes strayed in John, Lord Branton's direction.

It had been years since their last dreadful meeting. She had been a winsome girl visiting at Fairlea, and he a lovestruck youth with only the promise of the broad chest and shoulders from which she could hardly keep her eyes tonight.

They had thought they were in love, and then Lord Harry Fotheringay had come to visit his brother and had swept her off her feet with his dashing London ways. . . .

Resolutely she put them both from her mind. The past was past, and better left alone. Sarah was the focus of her life now, and Hassan Triste about to become a secondary one if it looked as if he were any danger to her niece's heart.

Chapter Eight

⟨❧⟩

EARLIER, SARAH HAD SAFELY SENT HALEY TO BRANTON House with her request that Jack come to talk over a matter of some importance, as she and Pen had decided. Now she was putting the finishing touches on the floral arrangements that would grace the formal rooms of Fairlea.

Cutting the flowers and making up the vases to brighten the various rooms of her home were the only two domestic duties her cousin had left to her.

Letticia was afraid of bees.

She was placing the last spike of blossoms, and thinking how much she enjoyed the quiet and cool of the flower room off the scullery when she heard a stifled sound behind her.

She whirled around.

William, his face pale and tear-streaked, stood in the doorway. Carsonby loomed behind him, his lean, dour face grim with concern.

With a cry of distress, Sarah sank to her knees on the wooden grating that formed a false floor above the drains of the flower room. Heedless of the damp that marked her skirt and the unevenness of the grid that bruised her knees, she opened her arms to the boy.

Sobbing, William threw himself into them.

Sarah's gaze flew to the butler's face seeking some explanation.

Carsonby shook his head, his lips a tight line.

Sarah held William even tighter. "What is it, William? What is wrong, dearest?"

William pulled his face away from her neck and looked over his shoulder at the doorway.

Sarah understood and motioned for Carsonby to leave them.

When he had gone, William, shivering hard, told her, "I think that my milk was poisoned last night." His eyes filled his face.

"Dear God!" Frantically she began to touch him on every limb, as if by checking them she could reassure herself that he had not been poisoned.

"N-no, Sarah. I didn't drink any." Tears of fright spilled down his cheeks. "B-but it was a very near thing."

"Oh, my darling, how terrible." She rose as she said it. Dread filled her.

First the bridge, and now this.

William regarded her through eyes that held a fear too large for a small boy to bear. His voice dropped to a broken whisper. "S-Sarah." Horror filled the room in which they stood as he said, "That isn't all."

His face went so white Sarah was afraid he would faint. Gathering him close, she staggered out of the flower room with him in her arms. She was driven to get him to a warmer place.

Cold fear made her clumsy as she rushed to the library.

She encountered a worried Carsonby the moment she reached the main hall.

He took the child from her in spite of her protests. Grimly he carried the boy close behind her to the library.

Sarah fell into a chair near the fireplace and reached out for William.

The butler put him in her lap. Taking a moment to poke up the fire and add two logs, he tried unsuccessfully to pretend he was not affected by the boy's terrible sobs. He offered in a low voice, "I can make hot chocolate and bring it myself."

Sarah nodded.

William was so tense his little body vibrated. He started when Carsonby shut the door behind him.

"William, dearest." She smoothed his hair back from his forehead and kissed him there tenderly. Sarah waited, worried and confused.

"Last night the new housekeeper, Mrs. Nethers, brought my glass of milk instead of Vera," William began.

Sarah knew that Vera took care of the Viscount, and that the boy was particularly fond of her. The statement obviously had some significance, but she couldn't fathom what it might be.

She waited for him to go on.

Carsonby came back with the hot chocolate almost immediately.

"Thank you, Carsonby." Sarah couldn't smile.

Carsonby left the room with obvious reluctance.

William shifted on her lap, but did not volunteer to take a chair of his own.

Touching his cheek, Sarah found it chilled in spite

of the mildness of the day. "Let's sit on the hearth rug, shall we, dear?"

He nodded and slipped down from her lap. She settled beside him close to the fire.

Handing him his cup, she urged, "Drink a bit of this and then you can tell me. I am worried, you are so cold. The chocolate and the fire should help, and then we will talk."

"I don't want to go home." He lifted pleading eyes to her.

"Drink some chocolate, please, dear. Then you must tell me all."

She saw his lips were almost blue. She must get him warm before she let him go further into whatever had frightened him.

She reached out and gathered him close to her side. William leaned against her as unbending as an oak. She could feel little shivers pass through him at intervals.

Sarah fought the feeling of helplessness that washed over her.

William steadied as he drank his chocolate. After he had drunk a bit of it, he sat up away from Sarah and shifted so that the fire toasted his back and he could look at her.

Though he was pale and tense still, he was no longer terrified. She smiled tentatively, her eyes grave.

Tightening his grip on his cup, he told her, "I don't like Mrs. Nethers."

Sarah knew there was more to come than dislike of the new housekeeper Jervase had installed. She kept silent.

"When she brought me my milk instead of Vera,

it made me angry." He didn't look the least bit repentant about it.

Sarah fought the desire to bite her lip to keep from urging him to go on and continued to wait quietly. Instead, she clenched her teeth to keep from speaking.

"She wouldn't leave, Sarah. She wanted me to drink my milk while she was there. She wanted it so bad her eyes gleamed with it." He shuddered at the memory.

"I pretended to take a swallow and looked at her like I wanted to be private, until she finally left. Then I put the milk down where Vera could take it away in the morning." His eyes flashed. "I didn't want any old milk from that woman."

William's anger faded, and his eyes grew wide again as he remembered. His voice was hesitant, his words slow. "Bathsheba was on the foot of my bed. She had jumped up there to chase Fluff down and stayed just for spite."

Sarah saw him quiver slightly and reached out and took his hand.

"Then Bathsheba got up and stepped all over me to go over and drink some of my milk."

"And . . . and in just a few minutes . . ." His eyes filled with frightened tears, and his voice quavered to a halt. It was a while before he could go on. "Bathsheba dropped down and meowed and shook a bit, and . . ."

His voice fell to a tremulous whisper Sarah could hardly hear. Spasms of fright shook him. "And she *died*."

"Oh, William!" Sarah let go of her cup, chocolate

splashing over her skirt, and snatched him into her lap. "My precious friend." She hugged him fiercely.

No child should ever look this way. Before her very eyes something of William's childish faith in the intrinsic goodness of the world had been stripped away.

Frantically she reassured him. "Bathsheba was a very old cat, you know." Even as she spoke, her mind accepted the distinct possibility that she was deceiving him.

She reached for anything that might comfort him—he needed all the comfort she could give. "Why, she was a cat full-grown long before you were ever born. She must be . . . have been . . . at least seventeen. It was past time for her to die, you know. She should not have been jumping up on beds or chasing Fluff. She was very old. So very old."

She could feel him considering her words and held her breath, praying he would accept them.

She held him tight as he began to relax against her and knew he was trying hard to believe what she had told him. Trying desperately to believe that his milk had not been poisoned.

With all her might she willed him to believe it. To forget the horror that had held him.

Finally he looked up at her hopefully. Anxiety and his terrible need to believe her tightened his face. "So it *wasn't* my milk?"

With no regard for whatever the truth might be, she said firmly, "Of course not, my angel. She was just a very old cat."

"Oh, Sarah." His face lit up. "That feels *so* much better!"

Sarah sent prayers of thanks winging upward,

and hugged him hard. Tears of relief formed behind her eyes.

No child should feel so bereft and alone. If there were danger, it was up to her to keep it from him.

"So I suppose I must go home again?" he asked quietly, pulling gently away from her.

In spite of her joy at the calm acceptance in his eyes, her heart wanted to cry out that he must not. That she would not let him.

To do so, however, would undo all that she had just accomplished to defeat the nightmare in his mind. That, she knew, must not happen.

She must plan. She must find a way to keep him with her that would preclude anyone making him go back to Althurst after today.

Jervase *was* his legal guardian, after all.

Sarah's mind worked quickly. While she did not particularly admire Jervase, she could not picture him so foolish as to try to harm William.

He would immediately be suspect. Everyone knew that he was the next in line for the title.

Did someone actually *want* to harm William? Was the accident at the bridge aimed at him? Or *was* it random mischief?

Was the milk poisoned? Or had she inadvertently struck on the truth when she suggested that the cat had died of old age?

Bathsheba had made the leap to the high bed and chased Fluff down, after all. Perhaps it *had* been too much for her ancient heart.

Sarah's stomach felt as if it were tying itself into a knot as she pondered it all. Why, oh why could not she be certain of what was going on?

Oh, Dearest God! Please help me to know what to do!

In her lap, she twisted her hands, a gesture hitherto foreign to her. She was fast learning what the vicar meant when he mentioned "an agony of the spirit." She felt as if her mind might burst from her concern for William.

She needed help. She didn't trust herself to do this alone. She vowed to seek out her aunt. They must formulate a plan to keep William safe as quickly as possible.

She smiled a bright, false smile at William. "Are you hungry?"

It was merely a rhetorical question, of course. William, in common with all little boys his age, was always hungry.

At his ready assent, she said, "Wonderful. Then do me a favor and run ask Cook to make a picnic for three." She marveled at his eagerness; truly children were resilient little people! "I'll send a note to Althurst telling them I've invited you to stay for lunch, and you and I will take Aunt Pen out to the temple on the lake. Would you like that?"

With a grin, William ran off to the kitchen. Obviously, he had cast aside his horrors. It had needed only Sarah's assurance that everything was all right.

Sarah's smile faded the moment he left the room. She listened to the clatter of his running feet until she could hear it no more.

She sat for a little time longer staring into the fire with anxious eyes that did not see. The note to Althurst would have to wait a minute or two.

Just right now, Lady Sarah Constance Fotheringay was working hard at trying to dispel her own horrors.

Chapter Nine

SARAH VOLUNTEERED TO PUNT THEM OUT TO THE TEMPLE in the neat, flat-bottomed boat kept on the shore nearest the island. The little punt was moored there so that whoever wanted to go out to the pretty marble edifice could reach it.

Penelope and William sat amidships and guarded the huge picnic hamper Cook had given them, while Sarah struggled manfully with the long punting pole to push them out to the island.

William wore a pleasant smile, part expectation of their luncheon in the marble temple on its grass-smothered island, and part relief that Bathsheba had died of old age. He turned to Pen. "I say, isn't this splendid?"

Penelope eyed Sarah's chocolate-splashed skirt and distracted countenance and lied for him. "Yes, simply wonderful."

She was worried, truth to tell, but she would hardly cause a child distress by saying so. Instead she smiled down at the boy and asked, "Was the picnic *your* idea?"

But she didn't listen to his response. She knew that something must be dreadfully amiss if her usually fastidious niece had so forgotten herself as to neglect to change a dress over which she had quite obviously spilled her chocolate.

Penelope bided her time. Surely Sarah would disclose all once they reached the temple.

They disembarked, and the three of them dragged the boat a little way ashore to secure it. Sarah and Pen carried the heavy basket between them to the temple, and there on the round marble table in the center of the open room, William, standing on one of the marble benches around the table, unpacked it.

"Oooh, look! Here is ham. And a whole roast hen!" He plunked it down and dove back into the basket.

Penelope reached out and touched Sarah's shoulder, her eyes inquiring.

Sarah shook her head and frowned in William's direction.

The two women found and spread the clean linen cloth Cook had packed for them to picnic on, organized the bounty she had supplied on it, and the three of them set to with a will.

Penelope noted that her niece's appetite seemed forced and that as soon as William was engrossed in his share of the picnic, she gave up all pretense of eating. It was her turn to frown at Sarah.

"Hide your eyes, William," she instructed a little later as she snatched up the hard-boiled eggs. "Sarah and I shall hide these, and you shall have to find them. Won't that be fun?"

William looked a little doubtful, but obligingly put his head down on the table on his folded arms.

Penelope grabbed Sarah's hand and dragged her out of the temple. Once out of earshot, she hissed, "*What* is going on?"

"Is it so obvious that something has happened?"

"Oh, Sarah. Just look down at your dress. You would never have come out in that." She pointed at the chocolate stains that patterned the pale blue muslin. "Not unless you were half out of your senses for some reason."

"You are right, of course." Sarah stared at her skirt distractedly while Pen bent down and hid an egg in the grass at the foot of a sapling. "I am half out of my mind with worry over William."

"What has occurred?" Another egg behind a handy rock.

"I shall tell you when William is busy searching."

Hastily they hid the rest of the eggs, and Sarah called to William, "Ready! Come and see how many you can find. There are ten in all. See if you can find every one."

Pen told her, "There were only nine. Cook sent three for each of us."

"Better to have him search for a tenth egg than to try to send him away so I can finish what I must tell you."

Pen looked at her niece with a new appreciation. A slow smile appeared. "Sarah. You have told a lie!"

Sarah's face flushed. "Well, don't try to make it sound like a virtue, for Heaven's sake. Besides, your own claim the other night at the table of a letter I know you never wrote nearly knocked me off my chair. So you, of all people, have no reason to come all virtuous over me!"

"I wouldn't think of it. I am merely applauding your newly found social acumen."

Sarah glared at her favorite aunt.

Together they made their way back to the temple. Sarah could hear Pen chuckling.

William had warmed to the idea of an egg hunt in their absence. "May I go look now?" he asked eagerly, jam on his chin from one of Cook's raspberry tarts.

Sarah's heart went all soft. Gratitude at his return to the boy she knew threatened to overwhelm her. She picked up his napkin and wiped his chin. "Go to it, William!"

She watched him hare off and smiled. Then, suddenly, a movement across the stretch of water on the side of the temple farthest from the manor caught her eye. There was someone at the edge of the woods! Sarah held her breath. It was a man on a large black horse. She fought her inclination to stiffen and stare, forced herself to behave naturally.

Moving so that Penelope was between her and the figure on the distant shore, she said, "Pretend to talk to me."

Pen's eyebrows soared. "Pretend? Indeed, I can hardly wait to do so in earnest. Pray what is the trouble now?"

"There is someone in the trees over there watching us. No! Don't turn around."

"I had no intention of doing so. Who is it? Can you see?"

Sarah drew a careful breath and narrowed her eyes. "Yes. It is Mr. Triste."

"Oh. What do you suppose he is doing there? Can you watch him while you tell me what is going on?"

Sarah assented, then proceeded to tell her aunt

what had happened in the flower room and the library this morning.

"Oh, my dear. I am so sorry. How distressed you must have been." She looked to where William had just discovered the first egg they had hidden and returned his triumphant wave. "How fortunate that you were able to turn his mind from such suspicion."

"Until we can be sure that it *is* merely suspicion and not actual danger, we must devise a way to keep William safe." Sarah's voice was desperate. "You *will* help me think of a way to do so, won't you? This, on top of the accident at the bridge, has me frantic! I simply cannot bear to see him so frightened!"

"Of course I will help, Sarah," Pen promised.

Sarah watched the man across the lake. As well as she could tell, he seemed to be looking in their direction. Could he be the source of danger to William that she feared?

A fierce protectiveness welled up in her. She turned her gaze back to her aunt and vowed, "I *shall* keep him safe. I *must!*"

William came running just then. "I have found only nine eggs. I fear we shall never find the last one."

"Perhaps it rolled into the lake," Pen suggested glibly.

While Pen praised him for finding the nine, Sarah had the grace to blush over the imaginary tenth egg.

William was half asleep by the time they disembarked on the shore of the lake. Worn out with the fright he had had and the sleepless night it had engendered, he had been quite grumpy since Sarah had admitted to miscounting the eggs.

"That is not in the least like you, Sarah." He was exceedingly put out. "And a shabby trick it was too. I bet I hunted ten minutes after I found that ninth egg." He scowled at his dearest friend.

"Oh, I am quite sure that it was all of a quarter of an hour, at least," Sarah told him. "I hope you will be able to forgive me someday." She smiled at him charmingly.

He was not proof against her. "Very well." He tried to sound stern, but a yawn spoiled the effect. "But you must be careful never to do it again."

"I shall be careful."

In spite of his sleepy protest that he could ride, Sarah insisted on sending him home in a carriage with his pony Hercules tied on behind.

William was asleep before she had finished tucking the featherweight summer carriage robe around him. She pressed a kiss to his grubby cheek, told Winnie again how much she appreciated her accompanying him, and gave Haley the order to drive the young Viscount home.

Sarah and Penelope spent several hours casting about for and finally perfecting a plan. Several more hours were spent polishing the details.

By the time Sarah walked her aunt to the second-best guest bedchamber, they were both ready to drop.

"Rest well. We shall have to breakfast by six if we are to get it all done and be back here in time to receive Jack Branton."

"Indeed"—Pen stifled a yawn—"I shall have not the slightest difficulty following that suggestion." But some of her comfortable drowsiness had been stripped away by the mention of *his* name.

Pen and Sarah didn't come down for breakfast until past ten the next morning. Neither spoke until Carsonby inquired whether they would like coffee or tea.

"Coffee, please," they said in unison. And then they were smiling, and the butler relaxed and filled plates for them.

"We were going to get up early, as I recall," Pen said.

"Yes. Well. Winnie decided we must have our rest and forbade anyone to wake us. We shall just have to send messengers to do some of our intended errands, and scramble to get the rest done."

"Very well." Pen looked down at her riding habit. "At least I had Maude dress me properly."

Sarah smiled at her. "We shall have to go in person to the solicitor, and of course to the jeweler's to—"

She broke off, deciding it might not be wise to let Carsonby know that she was planning to sell her pearls. She had to in order to get the money to rent Beaulieu so that her aunt could take up residence there early.

Sarah had the present owner's consent to visit Beaulieu with the various people she had chosen to renovate and redecorate the lovely manor for the time Sarah would purchase the estate on her birthday. She must not stretch that permission to include her aunt's occupancy without offering them remuneration.

To gain the funds she needed, Sarah would have to sell the pearls her grandmother had given her when she had turned fourteen. Still three weeks from her nineteenth birthday, she had no other way to raise the needed funds.

She knew beyond the shadow of a doubt that Carsonby would never approve, however. The butler was as protective of the family's possessions as if they were his own. Touching the strand of pearls where they lay inside the collar of her riding shirt, she felt again the awful sense of loss she had experienced earlier when she had made the decision to sell them. Her grandmother had been so very dear to her, and she missed her as much as she missed her parents. Only for William would she part with her gift.

Feeling quick tears spring up, she blinked resolutely. William's safety was worth any sacrifice to her. She refused to sit here and entertain for even an instant this tendency to become a watering pot, no matter how she treasured the means to keep him safe.

Pen saw Sarah touch her pearls and understood her distress, but wisely forbore to comment. Rising, she said briskly, "Well, I am off to choose a mount. Come as quickly as you can, for we have no time to spare."

Her unnecessary reminder had the desired effect. Sarah was up in a flash and behind her immediately. With a back-flung "Thank you, Carsonby," again in unison, they left the cozy breakfast room.

The ride to the small town on the far side of Little

Fairview village took just slightly longer than half an hour, as Pen had chosen to ride another mare as highly bred as Cymbeline. Each sleek animal had decided before they exited the drive at Fairlea that the other would in no way precede her.

As a result, the ladies arrived at the jeweler's in flushed disarray, and had to hire two sturdy boys to walk their lathered horses.

"We have several errands to discharge," Sarah told the young men. "Be sure you do not let them drink until they are considerably cooled, and then no more than ten swallows with further walking between their next drink. I have no desire to harm my horses."

The older boy assured the other that Lady Sarah was *usually* very considerate of her cattle. His friend had looked rather skeptical of her last words in light of the obviously hard-ridden condition of the two mounts.

They took the mares down the street and back while Sarah watched before she was content to leave the boys with the care of them.

Pen was impatient. "The horses will be fine, Sarah. Those boys know how to earn a shilling. Come. We have much to accomplish."

There was a thunder of hooves as they entered the jeweler's, and both women looked up and were startled to see the mysterious Mr. Triste canter by.

The man who called himself Hassan Triste rode to the Globe and Thistle, an inn several doors down from the shop the ladies had entered. There he gave his reins to the hostler and cautioned him that his mount was a stallion.

"I'll have a care, sir," he was assured by the

ruddy-cheeked youth. Satisfied that the hostler was competent, the man called Triste turned his full attention to the matter at hand.

He had followed Sarah and her aunt at a distance all the way from Fairlea. Their headlong dash out of the drive and into the public road had intrigued him.

Since their mounts had claimed all of their attention, he had been at liberty both to admire their skill as equestriennes and to ponder the cause of their haste.

He was surprised that their errand turned out to be no more pressing than a visit to the jeweler's, however. He was curious. Sarah, he knew, would never lather a horse merely to select some trinket.

Pulling his watch from its pocket, he deliberately snapped its golden chain. With the watch and its broken chain held casually in his gloved hand he set about seeing to its repair.

Removing his tall, curly-brimmed beaver, he bowed his head and entered the low door of the jewelry shop. Inside, Sarah and her aunt were standing at the counter that ran the width of the far side of the room, their backs to the door.

The tiny silver bell tinkled merrily as the door brushed past the spring it was mounted on, but neither of the two ladies who held his interest turned from their business to see who had entered.

Moving soundlessly to a glass case on the counter that ran down the left side of the small room, he pretended to study the collection of snuffboxes there. Easily he overheard the low-voiced conversation Sarah held with the proprietor of the shop.

"Well, if that is all you can manage, I shall have to be content with it."

"Sarah!" Her aunt was indignant. "This man is a thief!" She flashed an indignant glance at jeweler. "She would get twice as much in London and you know it."

The jeweler made an obsequious gesture, hands pleading. "This is not London, milady."

"Have done, Pen." Sarah's face was set. "Very well, Mr. Fladly. My pearls are yours."

Fladly brought his cashbox up from under the counter, his smile smug. He opened the box and counted out a sum the man watching knew to be far below the worth of the glowing heap of pearls on the dark velvet.

The watcher's jaw tightened.

Sarah turned from the counter with the money in her hand and a stricken look on her face. Her companion was clearly furious. In their distress, neither looked his way.

The shop owner, rubbing his hands with satisfaction over the bargain he had just made, approached his new customer, the pearls in his pocket.

When he looked into the eyes of this next customer, his smile died a cruel death.

"I have a fancy," the tall, dark man said in a voice like ice, "to own the pearl necklace you have just acquired." His eyes, storm dark, bored into the watery ones of the little man before him.

"Oh, sir. I couldn't possibly let you have them. They are spoken for. Mrs. Hardesty has wanted them ever since Lady Sarah's grandmother gave them to the girl."

"I will give you half again what you paid for them. Be assured I intend to have them."

"But they are worth twice that!"

"So I surmise." His expression became menacing. "Your continued good health is of some worth, however, and I assure you I have no intention of giving you the true value of the necklace when you did not so oblige its rightful owner."

"M-my health?"

"Exactly. I am told that a good horsewhipping leaves a man in a somewhat weakened state. You do not strike me as robust even now. But you do put me strongly in mind of a thief in sore need of a harsh lesson."

The jeweler stared into the implacable face above him. There he read a purpose that totally unmanned him.

"Here, here." Almost gibbering, he pulled the string of pearls from his pocket with a hand that shook. "Here. They are yours for the price I paid for them." He backed away until his back hit the wall.

"I will not cheat you of my offer, you worm." He counted out the pound notes he had promised. Fighting an urge to throw them on the floor, he held them out.

The jeweler took them carefully, as if he suspected they would burn his fingers. At the same time, he stepped forward and spilled the shining pearls into their new owner's waiting hand.

"Wa-was there something you wanted when you came in?" he quavered, shrinking away from this formidable man. He devoutly hoped the man would forget whatever he had entered the premises for and just leave.

"Nothing. I shall take care of the matter else-where."

Weak with relief, Mr. Fladly sagged against the counter for support until the last tinkling echo of the silver bell on the door had died. Then he took a deep breath and scuttled toward his living quarters behind the shop calling plaintively for his wife.

Chapter Ten

JOHN—JACK TO HIS FRIENDS—LORD BRANTON, WAS IN his study scowling over his bailiff's accounts when his friend arrived. He rose from his desk with a welcoming smile.

His visitor failed to return his greeting, demanding instead, "Where is the brandy?"

John gestured toward a drink table beside the door, and watched his friend almost fill a goblet.

Looking up from the task, he inquired, "Would you care for any?"

Lord Branton nodded, and his guest splashed a more normal quantity of the aromatic, golden liquid into a second goblet and carried both to the desk. Handing his host's to him, he flung himself into the chair in front of the desk and buried his nose in his own.

Jack laughed, a short, harsh sound, as if he were not quite on easy terms with laughter. "Well, I am relieved to see you have not picked up an aversion to good brandy during your sojourn in the abstentious land of the Muslims."

Seeing his friend's face close, he apologized immediately. With a helpless gesture he groaned, "God, I'm sorry, old man. It was just a stupid joke."

Eyes dark with remembered pain, the other said in a voice utterly devoid of emotion, "I take no offense, Jack. Do not trouble yourself."

Branton squirmed inside. How could he so callously have brought to mind the years of his good friend's bitter captivity? Striving to distract him, he asked, "Have you decided to accept my hospitality?"

Lifting his booted feet to rest on the already scarred edge of the desk, his friend replied thoughtfully, "If you are sincere in your desire to have me and understand that it will probably open you to all sorts of prying questions, then I shall come."

Rather than endure his host's glad reaction, he said, "Jack, I have just done something disgusting."

Jack looked hard at him, startled.

"I have bullied a worm, and feel filthy about it."

"Explain."

His friend shook his head without looking at him and began to tell him instead of his plans to subsidize a jeweler he knew in London. "He is an honest man, and I want him to come set up his business here."

He told Branton that the man he wished to sponsor had expressed a desire to raise his large family in a place that would be healthier for them than the teeming capital.

Jack leaned a broad shoulder against the mantel and looked inquiringly at his guest. That he thought it strange that his friend should take such an interest in a tradesman was obvious.

It was equally obvious that his companion had said all that he intended to say on the subject.

He did not tell his host how he felt about the

present local jeweler. He refrained, too, from telling Jack that he had a distinct yearning to see the craven little man who had cheated Sarah forced to set up business far away.

Nor did he tell him about his own purchase of Sarah's pearls.

Lady Sarah and her aunt left the solicitor's office with the signed one-month's lease agreement for the manor house at Beaulieu safely in hand. "Well, it is certainly a relief to have this done."

"Indeed," Pen agreed. "The first part of our plan is now in place. I shall remove to Beaulieu first thing in the morning and we shall hope the rest will follow as easily."

Sarah signaled to the two boys walking their horses that they were ready to have them brought up. She was pleased to see that both mares had cooled out nicely, and that they looked a good deal more sensible than they had when she and Pen had ridden them away from Fairlea.

Pen gave each of the young men a shilling, and accepted the tall one's assistance in mounting. With a smile that left both boys dazzled, she led the way out of town.

The two women enjoyed their ride home and arrived at Fairlea in plenty of time to change for the expected arrival of Lord Branton.

While she was bathed, Sarah pondered the wisdom of warning Pen that Jack was not overencumbered with the social graces to which Penelope was accustomed in the London gentlemen of her acquaintance. Sighing deeply, she finally decided that her aunt was perfectly capable of—in fact could hardly avoid—discovering this for herself.

The next problem, of course, was whether or not to prepare her aunt for disappointment in the event that Jack declined to come at all.

Dressed and on her way to the drawing room, Sarah met her aunt in the hall. She noted how lovely she looked in her simple gown, and found herself wondering how her taciturn friend Jack would react to her beautiful aunt.

In spite of her constant fear for William, it looked as if it were going to be an interesting afternoon.

"I simply *cannot* understand why you are being so mulish!" Penelope's face was flushed with anger as she glared at Lord Branton.

"Madame," he said coldly, black brows drawn down fiercely, "Pray calm yourself. I am not being recalcitrant. It is merely that all you have said, while alarming, does not conclusively prove that there is really a threat to the young Viscount."

"Dense!" Penelope stamped her foot and whirled away from him. "The man is dense!" She went to the window and presented her back to the two other occupants of the room.

Sarah stared at them in amazement. Everything was topsy-turvy! She had expected Jack to be difficult, but he was merely being cautious. She had further expected Pen to charm him to their aid, persuading him to find out why Triste was here, but Pen was . . .

She wasn't even certain *what* Pen was. Impatient with Branton's quiet, methodical review of the situation, certainly. She decided to leave it at that. It seemed the kindest course. Never would she want to call her aunt's behavior . . . unreasonable.

Even when it was.

As it was now.

She tried for order. "The matter is simple. We, too, are not *certain* that William is in danger." She heard her aunt snort. Shock momentarily immobilized her tongue, and she could only stare at the hearty gentleman opposite her.

Surely Aunt Penelope was incapable of such a sound! Pen was the receptacle of all graces.

Jack Branton threw a disapproving glance in the direction of the window at which Pen stood and said to Sarah, "Pray continue. I am certain we will be able to come to some useful conclusion now."

Penelope's back stiffened at his implication that her absence from the conversation would simplify it. For a moment Sarah was afraid she would come back into the discussion railing.

Never had she seen her sophisticated aunt so out of countenance. Indeed, Jack's mere presence seemed to have put Pen completely out of sorts.

Sarah recommenced with the distinct feeling that she was walking across thin ice in smooth-soled dancing slippers. "We"—she refused to exclude Pen, no matter the consequences—"had hoped to enlist you to discover who this Mr. Triste is, and just what he is doing in the neighborhood."

When the plural pronoun failed to draw more than a darkling expression from Jack, she went on with greater confidence.

"Nothing like what is now occurring in the neighborhood ever happened before he appeared,

Jack." She strove to make him see why his cooperation was essential. "And you must admit the circumstances surrounding him are suspicious in that he is a mystery."

Jack was absolutely silent for a long pause. Then he asked tentatively, "Why do you say so?"

"Because he is not an Arab. Neither is he French."

"How do you know?" Branton's brow took on a fine sheen of perspiration. "His name might suggest that he is perhaps the son of an Arab mother and a French father."

From her place at the window, Penelope sniffed loudly.

"Well, he is not." Sarah's tone brooked no argument.

"Why do you say so?" Branton was annoyed to find he was repeating himself. He took refuge in logic. "If you have no knowledge of the man's identity, surely you can have no knowledge of his antecedents."

Sarah found Jack's logic as irritating as Penelope had and snapped, "I simply know that he is, in spite of his appearance, English."

Jack stared at her.

She turned away from him and reached out to touch the wing of one of the Queen Anne chairs beside the fireplace. Taking a deep breath, she said, "I know that it sounds silly, Jack, but I have this strange certainty that I can trust him."

She traced the pattern of the brocade on the high back of the wing chair in front of her with her finger. She gave the matter so much concentration that she missed Branton's odd look.

"It is almost as if I know him." She turned back to

face him. "But of course, I do not." She threw her hands wide and began to pace the room. "It is a most vexing situation, and coupled with my fear for William's safety, it is about to drive me frantic. That is why you must help."

Lord Branton's dark eyebrow rose, but he did not speak. A single bead of sweat trickled down his left temple.

Sarah tried to explain patiently. "You are the friend who introduced him into the midst of us. Since you haven't volunteered any information about him during our talk, I can only surmise that you don't know much more than we do."

Still he didn't comment.

Penelope swept back to them, her own patience clearly exhausted. "Obviously Lord Branton does not care to place himself at our disposal, Sarah." She looked at the man as if he were repugnant. "*His Lordship*"—she made the form of address insulting— "must feel that the safety of his young neighbor is none of his affair, and best left in the hands of two frail women."

Anger lit Jack Branton's fine brown eyes. "Now, see here, Penelope. I have made no such pronounce-ment. In fact, I have said little. All my energy has been spent trying to ascertain . . ."—he took a ragged breath and plowed on— "whether or not I am dealing with the foolish imaginings of silly women."

Penelope clapped a hand to her bosom and gasped for air.

Sarah blinked and fought down a strong resent-ment that gushed up in her with the force of an artesian well.

"Jack!" Sarah cried forcefully, torn between her

own offense and her eagerness to capture his attention before Penelope recovered sufficiently to find words with which to express *her* outrage. "How can you say that? You know perfectly well that I have always been perfectly sensible! You should beg our pardon."

Out of the corner of her eye she saw Pen taking long, steady breaths to calm herself while her eyes seemed to shoot sparks at the large, robustly handsome man she yearned to annihilate.

Jack ignored Penelope while he interrupted Sarah in order to put her at her ease. "Sarah, I would not have agreed to come here today if I did not intend to help you. Just give me a few days, and I promise I shall come to you with Hassan Triste's full story."

"We truly are not being . . ." Sarah couldn't finish her sentence.

"Silly?" Jack, hoping to distract her from her investigation of his houseguest, supplied with helpful stupidity.

Pen's breathing took on a hissing sound as she inhaled through clenched teeth.

Sarah flinched. Oh, why must Pen and Jack get along like a pair of cats? Everything would be so much simpler if they just weren't so at odds with each other!

Jack looked her way with calm interest. "No, Sarah. I don't think *you* are ever silly." His eyes returned to the delectable Penny. *Oh, hell. In for a penny, in for a pound!* "I have no idea, however, whether or not your deductions had been influenced by a less stable party."

Pen's lovely eyes fairly started from their sockets. She had not lived in Town for the past ten years without learning to govern her tongue. Somehow, however, she seemed to be having less than success with her temper for the first time in many years.

Smiling with bright falsity, and with each word as brittle as the ice it resembled in temperature, she finally managed a response. "How exceedingly kind of you," she enunciated with killing clarity, "to chance allying yourself with two such hen-witted females." She glided toward him with the grace of a hunting cheetah. "I declare you the very model of all that is to be desired in a gentleman to so imperil your reputation over a matter so insignificant"— her voice strengthened—"*as the safety of a mere child!*"

Sarah gasped at the insult to their guest even as she marveled at the deadly travesty of a smile her aunt offered Jack. Never had she seen her beloved aunt behaving so like a cross between an avenging angel and a . . . a harpy!

Never had she seen *anyone* so insult a guest!

She turned apprehensive eyes toward Jack, but he merely regarded Penelope calmly. He continued to do so until Sarah thought she would scream.

She thought, too, that Pen would soon be experiencing some small discomfort in the way of dryness to the surfaces of her blazing green eyes if she didn't relent and blink.

Obviously, her aunt was refusing to surrender in what she clearly considered a battle of wills.

Finally Jack's gentlemanly instincts won out over his enjoyment of the glorious creature's fine, if furious, eyes and he released her by looking back at the girl he had known all her life.

"Very well," he said briskly. "I shall report back when I have talked this over with H-Hassan."

The two women stared at the doorway through which he departed and listened until the sounds of his bootheels faded away into silence.

Seriously, Sarah contemplated her aunt. The strangely heightened feelings that had given this debacle its odd quality nagged at her. She had the uncomfortable feeling that Aunt Pen and Jack had been *not saying* much more than they had said. The whole exchange had had the curious quality of the half farce, half dream. Or nightmare.

The only conclusion Sarah could draw was that somehow, sometime, Pen and Jack had known one another before, and that the tensions of today's strange encounter were the result of that past meeting.

Simply nothing else would explain it.

Chapter Eleven

❧❧❧

GETTING PEN SETTLED AT BEAULIEU WAS OF PARAMOUNT importance. She must be in residence there as soon as possible so that there would be a safe place for Sarah to hide William, as she and Pen had planned. Maude was already there supervising the dusting.

To that end, an expedition had been scheduled for seven o'clock this misty morning. One of the maids would be bringing Pen her chocolate at six, so that Sarah's abigail, Winifred, might have her dressed in time to go to Beaulieu with them.

Sarah hoped idly that Winnie wouldn't drive Pen frantic whispering, "Bow—like in your hair—lee, yer: crammed together quick like. Bow-lee-yer." The plump lady's maid had been reminding herself at intervals of the proper pronunciation.

Since Winifred had learned she was shortly to make Beaulieu her future home, she had embarked on a mission to see that everyone said it correctly. Now that she knew, she had scant patience when the other servants called it Bewley.

Today, however, Sarah couldn't be bothered with that. She had something that she must get done before the house awakened to mount the expedition to the neighboring estate. To accomplish it, she rose well before dawn and dressed herself in her best riding habit.

Today was Hugh Warren's birthday, and she was going, as she always did, to put flowers on his grave. Others would come from Althurst to do the same later in the day, but this time was hers alone.

Sarah always came by herself. Never able to sort out the feelings that assailed her at his graveside, she was reluctant to have anyone observe her there.

The early morning mist swirled high and thick around her as she approached the tall granite monument that stood over Hugh's empty grave. Shining weakly through the gossamer banners of the mist, the barely risen sun touched and picked out in fitful light that carved design on the bas-relief shield that bore Hugh's coat of arms.

She stood for a moment looking at the riot of yellow and purple-faced wild pansies that pressed against the base of the monument. Heartsease.

She felt no ease in her own heart as she laid the heavy sheaf of flowers she had brought at the base of the monolith and stepped back away from it. Standing there, she thought of him and her heart tightened in her chest.

Hugh.

Her friend.

She wondered if she would ever get over losing him.

He had been the only person to whom she had ever confided her tearing sense of loss after the death of her parents. And Hugh, who had never suffered loss, or known unhappiness, had somehow understood and made her feel she could go on.

She brushed away the single tear that had escaped her lashes, then sighed, and turned away to mount her mare.

Gathering up her reins, she asked Cymbeline, "Why is it that my prayers are always to keep Hugh safe? Why do I never pray that God grant him rest?"

The mare nickered softly, as if she would answer, then, uncharacteristically, moved calmly off toward their destination.

Neither mare nor mistress saw the tall man and his black horse that seemed to blend and fade until they were part of the heavy mist on the other side of the granite monument.

Later in the morning, Sarah and Pen in company with their escorts, Jack Branton and the mysterious Mr. Triste, rode to Beaulieu to await the arrival of the servants and the few pieces of furniture that were Sarah's and Pen's. The morning had cleared off beautifully, and the ride over from Fairlea had been much more pleasant than Sarah had expected it to be. She was glad the reservations she had had when she was informed that the two men were waiting to accompany them had proved unwarranted.

Pen rode with Mr. Triste just behind Sarah and Jack. Once or twice Sarah heard him laugh—a low, quiet laugh that held a tinge of . . . of what?

How could she think that laughter could hold a hint of sadness? But she heard it in his, and wondered if that was the reason for the twinge she felt.

Surely she was not *envious* that it was Pen who had drawn him to laugh and not she! Certainly not!

Never had she been prey to petty jealousy, and she was not about to be prey to it now.

"Sarah, why are you blushing?" Jack was looking at her curiously. He always had seen more than most men of her acquaintance. Until now, Sarah had always found that an admirable trait.

"It is the sun. The day has turned out to be warmer than I had expected when I dressed this morning."

"Let's stop and you can take off that jacket."

"No, thank you. I shall be fine." She would be too. Just because she felt a strong pull of some sort from the man called Triste didn't mean she was going to let it affect her behavior.

It was merely that her nerves were in tatters from her trip to Hugh's gravesite. They always were, no matter how many years passed. She wondered if she would ever accept the fact that he was gone.

Resolutely she turned her thoughts away from the tiny ache in her heart and set herself to be as entertaining to Jack as Pen was so obviously being to the man behind her. Ugh! There she was again being snide—or at best less than gracious—because she was . . . Was what?

She told herself again that it was merely her nerves. This time she assured herself that they were on edge because of yesterday's *contretemps* between her aunt and Lord Branton.

She heard her teeth grate, then found herself prattling. "This is ever so nice of you, Jack. And you, too, Mr. Triste." She glanced back over her shoulder to accept Triste's gracious nod. "But it really isn't necessary, you know. I have been to the manor several times alone to see what must be done, and have never had the least fright."

"Sarah," Jack said sternly, "with all the soldiers returning from the Continent on half pay or none at all, that could be dangerous. An empty house might seem to some of them a good place to rest on their way home. For a lovely young lady to go into one unescorted is extremely foolish."

Sarah struggled to focus on the compliment tucked away in his scold. Hearing the word "foolish" again after the feelings it had ignited yesterday did not appeal to her.

Most especially, she hoped Pen would not again take offense at the plainspoken Branton. Pen, however, was busy in an attempt to learn something of the man at her side. "Have you been in England long, Mr. Triste?"

"I returned two months ago after a protracted absence." He answered graciously enough, but his words gave very little information, and his tone indicated that he was not going to elaborate.

Pen was not, in spite of Jack Branton's intimations, foolish. She gave up. The rest of her conversation she kept to mere pleasantries.

Jack interrupted Sarah's thoughts. "After we have seen that the house is safe for you and Lady Penelope, H-Hassan and I will check out the stables for you, Sarah." He had a sudden thought. "Unless, of course, you want to go through the gardens with him. He is a fine gardener."

Sarah looked with startled interest at Triste. "A gardener?" Her voice reflected her surprise.

Triste smiled a twisted smile at her incredulous tone. "A gardener, Lady Sarah." His eyes burned for an instant, and Sarah wondered if he had recalled some unpleasant memory connected with his gardening.

"Splendid," she managed, her breath trapped in her throat by the intentness of his gaze. "I love flowers, but I really know nothing about growing them. I've always wanted to learn, but there never seemed to be time for it."

"I shall be pleased to share what I have learned with you, milady." His voice sounded as tight as his offer did formal.

Sarah wondered if she were imagining some sort of stress in Mr. Triste's manner, but their arrival in the open forecourt of Beaulieu manor forestalled any pursuit of the matter.

"Why, Sarah, it is absolutely beautiful!" Pen's throaty little voice was full of admiration.

"Yes, isn't it?" Sarah sighed. "I hope to come to love it as I have always loved Fairlea."

Triste turned toward her, his face serious. "The home of one's birth must always occupy a special place in one's heart, Sarah." He spoke with such sincerity that she barely noticed he had addressed her without her title. "The love you will lavish upon Beaulieu will make it special too."

Sarah's throat constricted. For just a fleeting instant, she was reminded of the way Hugh had always found the right words to comfort her.

Hugh had never spoken in the stilled fashion of the man before her, however. Triste spoke as if his English had somehow fallen into disuse, and was not yet coming to him with what Sarah was certain was his former fluency.

How she longed to solve the mystery of this man!

She shook her head to rid her mind of the fancies brought on by her visit this morning to her missing friend's grave. She squeezed her eyes tightly closed and willed herself to forget her foolish longing for someone she still held dear who had probably died years ago.

When she opened them, Triste had dismounted and stood close by Cymbeline, ready to help Sarah down. She unhooked her knee from her leaping horn so that she might slip from her saddle and placed her hands on his broad shoulders. Before she could slide down, he took hold of her waist, lifted her down and set her gently on her feet.

She knew from the look in his eyes that he saw her inner turmoil as clearly as if she wore a sign. Gratitude welled up in her to see that he had no intention of inquiring into it.

His touch sent little waves of awareness through her. She found she was hard put to keep her voice steady as she said, "Thank you."

Eyes darkened with some emotion, his gaze locked with hers. "Shall we explore your gardens?"

Sarah nodded, not trusting herself to speak. She felt as if his hands had crushed the breath from her lungs, yet his grip had been light.

Why did this man's touch cause such a reaction in her? Jervase and a dozen other men frequently helped her down from a horse's back without occasioning a single . . . A single what?

She couldn't even put a name to the sensation that still rippled through her. Troubled, she led the way off the paved forecourt into the gardens that surrounded the mansion, eager to divert her thoughts.

Triste, after walking beside her quietly, waiting,

she knew instinctively, for her to recover herself, began showing her the contents of what was soon to be her garden. "Weeds seem to be taking over," he said mildly, "but if you look you will see that there are many fine plants here." He used the crook of his horn-handled hunting crop to lift aside a wild vine and show her the rosebushes it concealed.

"I have always been particularly fond of roses." She removed one riding glove to touch the velvet of a blossom.

"I know."

She was startled. "You know? How can you possibly know my preference in flowers?" Sarah stared at him in consternation.

"All women favor roses, Sarah." His eyes were veiled.

"Yes, of course." But she kept looking at him a long moment.

He broke the strange tension between them by saying, "And here are iris . . . and peonies." He indicated light green blade-shaped leaves that thrust up out of the weeds like swords and large mounds of dark green foliage. Both held evidence of spent blossoms.

He led her through the garden that was soon to be hers, and recited a quiet litany of the plants that he found there. His voice was as impersonal as any lecturer's, but his eyes . . .

Sarah fought for a moment to pin down what she felt about his eyes. Finally she decided it was better simply not to look into them.

She tried, too, not to wonder how such a man became knowledgeable about gardens. He seemed more a warrior to her—he was so quick, alert, powerful—than someone who cared about gardens.

Sarah, who had never felt odd in the presence of any man, was a little nervous to be alone with this one. That Pen and Jack had gone to look at the house made her feel as if there were no one else in the world. Just herself and this man with the mesmerizing blue eyes.

Sarah burst into laughter when he began giving her detailed instructions for the application of compost and mulches. "Please! My poor head is spinning. I hope you will be so kind as to repeat all this wisdom to the gardeners I shall hire." She hated the way her words were practically falling over one another. "Rest assured, if it were left to me to do all this, I should probably tear out the flowers and preserve the weeds, for to my untutored eye they are obviously the healthier looking."

It was Triste's turn to laugh. "Yes." His eyes, however, avidly studied her averted face, and there was no laughter in them—only an aching tenderness.

"How many gardeners do you think I shall need?"

He told her with quiet assurance, "I shall take care of the matter for you, Sarah."

The huskiness in his voice startled her into looking straight at him. For a breathless moment, Sarah forgot the impropriety of letting a man she did not know offer to perform a service of such magnitude for her.

For that isolated space of time she saw only his eyes and felt only a strange, poignant yearning.

When she could speak, there was nothing she could think of to say but "Thank you."

And there it was again, that smile that had so changed him when they had met at the bridge—and he had caught and held her in his arms to keep her safe.

Suddenly, a swirl of so many emotions tangled in her chest that, drowning in them, she sought refuge in the first thing that came to her mind. "William. I must ride to Althurst and tell William I shall be here at Beaulieu from now on."

The tenderness he had tried to hide from her surfaced briefly. "You truly care for the young Viscount."

"Of course!"

"He is happy?" The question was guarded.

"No." She answered reluctantly, sorry it was so and sorry to tell him. She drew her soft leather riding glove through her bare hand.

"Ahhh." The sound held pain.

Sarah wondered that she didn't find it odd, this inescapable sharing of her private thoughts with a man she barely knew. Now, she found herself offering him solace. "But the staff at Althurst loves him dearly, and so do I."

From Triste, it brought a smile. "How fortunate he is to have you as his champion, Sarah."

"Thank you."

His eyes saddened, and he seemed to look inward. "When I was young," he said slowly, looking off into the distance, "I lived in a happy home, surrounded by people who loved me. Very precious among them was a young friend"—he looked back at her—"who needed me."

Sarah's breath caught in her throat.

His eyes seemed to fill with light then darken again as his words took on the peculiar quality she had noted before. "Such a beginning imbues one with the strength to endure life when adversity strikes and it becomes . . . unbearable."

He smiled a smile that nearly broke her heart. "I am glad that the young Viscount—" He broke off.

Sarah's lips parted, but under the spell of his eyes she forgot what it was that she had been going to say. Held by his gaze, she could only stand and let the feelings his nearness engendered sweep over her.

"—-that William has you."

Such was the spell in which he held her that she did not think it odd that he spoke with such familiarity of her young friend. She only wondered what power drew her next words from her. "As I had Hugh."

A blaze of joy lit his face, and he reached for her. Just short of crushing her in his arms, and even as she swayed to meet him, Sarah saw him reassert his iron will.

She drew herself back as well, with an effort that shocked her in its intensity. Would she really have let this stranger embrace her?

Her face flamed. Had she . . . actually *wanted him to*?

Gasping "I must go to William," she offered her errand as the excuse to quit his dangerous presence, and turned away. Walking briskly back to the forecourt where she had left her horse, she stumbled occasionally in her haste.

Reaching Cymbeline, she snatched her reins from

the ring of the horse-head hitching post and flung herself up into the saddle. She felt as if she were fleeing!

Cymbeline threw up her head and snorted. She had caught her mistress's mood. Sarah might only be running from emotions that threatened to overwhelm her, but the highly bred mare interpreted her rider's panic as imminent danger to them both. With an ear-splitting whinny, she tore away from the forecourt, her iron-shod hooves striking sparks from the paving stones.

The glance Sarah threw back over her shoulder as she turned her mare toward Althurst showed her the tall, solemn-faced Triste bending to retrieve the glove she had dropped in her haste to mount.

The speed with which Cymbeline galloped away carried Sarah into the woods. In full leaf, the thick trees quickly hid the tall man from view.

He stood stone-still, looking after her. He watched the place in the woods where he had last seen her for a long while. Then he raised the glove, still warm from Sarah's hand, and pressed it reverently to his lips.

Chapter Twelve

CYMBELINE TORE THROUGH THE WOODS, STORMED ACROSS
Fairlea jumping hedges at a full gallop, and thundered across the newly repaired bridge to Althurst.
Sarah let her run unchecked, reveling in the way the
mare's mood matched her own.

As she neared Althurst, she even imagined that
the mare's frantic pace was in answer to some silent
call from William. Tossing her reins to the groom
who had run to meet her, she leapt from the saddle
and rushed up the steps to where a footman held
the door open to receive her.

As she hurried through it she could see Grimsby,
a welcoming smile on his usually somber face,
coming across the enormous hall. "Grimsby, hello.
Where is William?"

"His Lordship is on the east terrace with his
spaniel, I believe, Lady Sarah."

"Thank you." Without waiting for his escort,
Sarah started for the terrace. As she passed under
the stair, she glanced up and saw the white, strained
face of Jervase's "housekeeper" looking down at her
from two floors above, her eyes malevolent.

The woman offended Sarah. Why, she had no
idea, for while it was rumored that the attractive

woman was Jervase's mistress, Sarah would have had to strive mightily to care whether or not it were so.

She just did not like the woman, and wished she were not at Althurst—probably because William took her in such dislike. It was William's house, after all. Jervase should send the woman packing.

Finally she reached the end of the hall and the lovely French doors that led out onto the east terrace. Through them in a flash, she smiled in anticipation of discovering William. "William!"

There was no answer to her call. At first glance the terrace seemed deserted. "William?" She looked anxiously around.

Her searching glance fell on a pile of rubble near the other end of the smooth-flagged surface. Her mind froze. Without thought she ran toward the heap of broken stone. "William! Oh, God! Where are you, William?"

There was a high whine, then a sharp bark.

"Fluff!" She whirled to see the fat little spaniel, clasped spasmodically in William's arms, struggle to get free to come to her.

William stared straight ahead with eyes that did not see her and clutched the dog all the harder.

Fluff yelped in protest.

Sarah threw herself to her knees and scooped William into her arms. "William, dearest. It's me, Sarah. I'm here, dearest. It's me."

Unyielding for the space of a breath, William suddenly burst into tears and clutched her wildly. "Sarah! Sarah!" His wails filled her ears.

She plopped gracelessly to the cool stones of the terrace and dragged him into her lap. She rocked with him, cuddling him and stroking his hair. "Ah, dearest, what is it?"

She threw a quick glance at the rubble on the flagstones and saw that it was all that remained of one of the huge stone ornamental urns that lined the edge of this section of the roof of Althurst manor.

Looking up, she saw the gap in their ranks on the roof edge where the smashed one had stood. A tremor shook her at the thought that William had been here on the terrace when it came crashing down.

Her arms involuntarily tightened around the child. She heard her own breath sobbing in her lungs over the soft crying of the boy.

Rage prickled up the back of her neck and along her scalp. Who had done this? In light of the other things that had occurred to frighten this precious child, Sarah had no doubt that this was a deliberate attempt on his life.

Without waiting to calm him further, she gathered him closer and lunged to her feet. She ran, staggering, down the shallow steps to the broad lawn.

Stumbling across the grass, she fell once to her knees. She was a small woman, and the boy was heavy for her. She would die before she put him down, however. William would not put foot to ground again until she, Sarah, had gotten him to a safe haven. She swore it!

Fleeing as if every window in the great house hid the eyes of a would-be murderer, she dove with him into the woods. Shoving her way through the low branches of young trees, she ran over the thick carpet of leaves until she could run no more.

Collapsing against the trunk of a mighty oak that had probably seen the Magna Carta Barons ride past, she finally looked into William's tearstained face. What she saw there tore at her heart.

She gently smoothed his tousled hair back from his forehead and asked between panting breaths, "Please try . . . to tell me . . . what happened, dear . . . est."

William only stared at her, his eyes huge in his frightened, still face.

Sarah patted his back and huddled close with him to give him a chance to recover while she got her breath back. When, at last, his rigid little body relaxed against her and he pushed his face against her throat, Sarah sighed with relief.

"William?"

"It was the urn." He said that and no more.

Sarah waited a long while. Then, "William, if you cannot tell me just now, I shall wait and hear later." She felt him stiffen again and hurried to reassure him. "But I do not want you to think that I shall ever leave you again. I will take you with me. Away from Althurst."

He pulled away from her far enough to look into her face. His eyes searched it relentlessly. Satisfied with what he saw, he sighed and tucked his head back under her chin.

Sarah sat and waited. After a while she straightened her cramped legs.

Her movement seemed to release something in William. "Sarah?" It was no more than a whisper.

"Yes, William?"

"I heard the stone of the urn make a grinding noise. You know. Like a mill wheel. And I looked up and I saw . . ." He gulped.

Sarah waited.

"I saw somebody push it down on me."

Sarah heard a whimper, and realized that it was her own. Her mind was in turmoil.

A great, blasting agony tore through her. Who could have done this horrible thing to an innocent child? The agony was followed by a rage greater than she would have believed herself capable of.

She tightened her hug and fought for control. "Could you see who it was, William?" She was amazed at the calmness of her own question.

"No," he said in a very small voice.

They sat there together for a while in silence. Then Sarah asked him very quietly, "William, can you stay here while I go get Cymbeline?"

His hands clutched at her and he clung fiercely. "Yes," he said through clenched teeth.

Sarah sat a while longer. When she felt him relax a little she said, "I shall be right back, William. Hide yourself well, hold on to Fluff, and watch for me to come. Whatever you do, do not come out of hiding until you are certain it is I."

He looked up at her with determination on his face. "I will hide well, Sarah. And I will not come out until I am certain that it is you and Cymbeline. I promise."

Sarah realized that she had inadvertently given him a task that steadied him and was glad. Putting him out of her lap, she accepted his assistance to rise, hugged him hard, and told him again, "I shall be right back."

Their gazes held for a moment, then she turned resolutely and walked briskly away in the direction of the house. Behind her she heard the whipping of branches as William scurried to do as they had agreed.

Entering through the same door through which she had reached the terrace, she composed her face carefully as she sped down the hall.

Grimsby met her in the great hall.

"I did not find William, Grimsby." At the butler's quick start of alarm, she placed a hand on his sleeve and looked around to be sure she was unobserved.

Almost certain there was no onlooker, she looked hard at the old man and shook her head ever so slightly. Her fingers bit into his sleeve. "Please have my horse sent round, Grimsby."

"Your horse, milady?" Grimsby knew that she always rode a mare, and never before had she failed to ask for her mount by name.

His eyes troubled, he told her, "I shall send for your *horse* immediately, Your Ladyship." He clapped his hands, and a footman leapt into view. "Her Ladyship's . . . horse."

The footman was gone in a flash to signal a groom to bring Sarah's mare around. While they waited, they stared into one another's eyes.

What Grimsby saw in Lady Sarah's made his blood run cold.

Chapter Thirteen

❦

HALEY REPORTED TO SARAH THE INSTANT HE RETURNED from Althurst. "Sorry it took me so long, Your Ladyship, but it was hard to get Grimsby alone. There's a right proper flap about the young Viscount not turning up. 'Specially after they found that mess on the terrace." He saw Sarah shudder and inwardly cursed at himself.

"But you *were* able to tell Grimsby that William is all right?" Sarah was terribly anxious about her old friend.

"Oh, yes. And he was mighty glad to have the word, I can tell you. Says please to keep him informed and to tell him if you need his help in any way. A fine old gent."

"Thank you, Haley."

"Aye, milady. And mum's the word."

"Indeed, yes! Please."

Sarah closed the door to Pen's boudoir carefully and turned back into the room. Leaning against the decorated white paneling of the door, she pulled the little tatters of her nerves together and concentrated on the tasks of the immediate future. After a brief tussle with her worries, she was able to smile at the scene before her.

Pen and Winnie had William standing on a stool in the center of the still scantily furnished room. Pen was pulling and pinning, while Winnie plied her needle to the hem of the dress they were fitting to the restless boy.

William had never looked so mutinous in all the years that Sarah had known him. The pleased laughter that had risen in her throat to see his disguise so complete died there when she saw the fire in his fine blue eyes. It would never do for her to fuel that flame into open rebellion.

"Oh, dear." She pushed away from the door and sped across the room to him. "Darling, it is for your safety. You must not mind. Surely it will only be for a little while."

Pen spoke around a mouthful of pins. "Of courf he doef not mind. Wearing a difguif to foil onef enemif if vaftly clever." She spat the pins into her hand. "That is to say, of course William does not mind wearing a disguise to foil his enemies. It is vastly clever of him to do so, and we shall have lots and lots of good laughs together about it later too." Pen smiled down at the boy.

William looked a little less mulish.

Pen pursued her advantage. "Won't it be fun to have everybody think you are my niece for a while?" She cocked her head. "Why, we shall have to go to tea at Fairlea where you will be able to sit about and be treated like a young lady guest instead of having to do the pretty as gentlemen must. And you will play that young lady to such perfection, I do not doubt for a moment that you shall fool them all!"

She placed another pin and turned him. "Just

remember that you are my niece come to stay with me until your parents get settled in their new plantation in the Colonies."

"Shall I have all the cakes I want?" William teased, keeping his mind on the really important things.

"Yes!" Pen sounded exasperated. "Just *please* don't forget who you are and why you are here, will you?"

"All right. Shall I have all the pastries I want if we go to tea at Fairlea? Rueben hasn't left there yet, and he makes the best pastries in the neighborhood."

Pen pretended to consider this, and then gave him the answer he wanted. Mutiny was averted and she was able again to fill her mouth with pins and get on with "Wilhelmina's" fitting.

Sarah watched, fascinated to see her aunt's skill at alteration. Then, quietly she asked, "Do you suppose you could remember to answer to Mina, William?"

"Why?" The frown was back.

"Well, if we call you Willy for short, it will make me nervous because it is too close to William."

"Then why did we choose Wilhelmina for my name?" William's voice was turbulent.

"Pttfftuf." Pen's pins came out again. "William, if you had thought about it, you would have been able to tell us the answer to that question yourself. It was because it would excuse any slips we might make." She smiled at him brightly. "By the time we get the 'Wil' out, you see, we will realize our mistake and be able to add 'helmina' to save the day.

"If we had chosen Joan or Mary, that simply wouldn't have worked." She placed the hand without pins on his shoulder. "At the same time, we certainly don't want to set people's minds searching for something familiar about you that calling you Wil might trigger, do we?"

Wisely, she forbore telling him that if he should be unmasked, he would be forced to return to Althurst. She was well aware that Sarah had been up several times in the night to calm the child's nightmares about things falling from the roof.

Sarah moved close and gave him a quick hug, being very careful of all his pins. "Just think of the wealth of tales we shall have to tell when this is all over!"

William stared at her owl-eyed. "Yes, Sarah. Though I, for one, am not at all certain that I should precisely like to tell tales in which I am hiding in *skirts*." He gave his graceful muslin gown a dissatisfied twitch.

He raised solemn eyes to the two beside him. "And I should so very much like to know," he said softly, his eyes pleading, "when will it *be* over?"

Sarah and Penelope looked at each other for a long moment. Each of them repressed a sigh. That, indeed, was the question. And as yet, neither one of them had an answer.

Jack stood in the middle of his study at Branton and shouted at the crestfallen groom. "What the devil do you mean he's disappeared?"

Beside him, white-faced, Triste waited, holding his breath, for the man's answer.

"Near as me and Larkin can make out, there was some sort of accident on the terrace."

Triste drew in his breath quickly.

"Somepin' dropped offen the roof, the maid I talked to did say. After that the Viscount went missing."

Jack tried to ask calmly, "What do you mean 'went missing'? Was the boy hurt?"

"No, Your Lordship, that ain't what I mean. He just warn't there no more. That nice Lady Sarah Fotheringay come to see him, and tells Grimsby— that's the butler—that she can't find the little tyke nowhere."

"What did Grimsby do?" Jack wondered worriedly how his friend kept his feet when his face was so bloodless.

"Well, he was all upset for a while. Then he come to himself, and he has 'em search the house from top to bottom, then he sends 'em out to scour the grounds. But they didn't find no sign of the lad. He was just gone."

"And you and Larkin and Simms saw nothing?"

"No, Your Lordship." He offered as if it were a peace offering, "But me and Simms got a good look at that there terrace, and there weren't no blood on it."

Jack saw Triste sway. "That will be all, Kemp." And as an afterthought, "Thank you."

Before the door had closed behind his man, Branton grabbed his friend by the arm and forced him into a chair. An instant later he pressed a glass of brandy into his hand.

Then he stood by helplessly and watched him try to come to grips with his pain. Finally, unable to bear it any longer without offering comfort, he burst out, "Hang on, Hugh. Hang on. I promise you we'll find him!"

*   *   *

When it was too dark to see their hands before their faces, Lord Branton pulled in his stumbling horse. In the dimness, he peered at the strained, set face of the Sixth Viscount Althurst.

"We're going in now, Hugh," he told him as if speaking to a child from whom weariness had robbed the power to comprehend. "We have combed every inch of the country for miles. Now even the horses can't see to find their way."

When his friend failed to answer him, Jack reached out and took the gelding Hugh rode by the bridle. Earlier, Althurst had ridden his stallion to the point of exhaustion, switched horses twice since, and had now reached that state himself.

Physically exhausted, worn out by the emotions that tore him apart, Hugh Warren, Sixth Viscount Althurst, allowed his friend to lead him back to Branton.

In the study, Branton shoved a glass of wine into his morose friend's hand. "Hugh, there is a chance that William was just badly frightened and that he fled to Sarah. He loves her best of anyone he knows. *And* he knows that she would protect him at any cost."

Light reentered Althurst's eyes. "Of course." His voice was hoarse with weariness. "Why did I not think of that?" His words gained strength as his spirit gained hope. "Surely he would flee to Sarah if he felt threatened." He made as if to rise from his chair.

Branton shoved him back. "No, Althurst. You cannot crash in on Sarah in the middle of the night. We will go in the morning."

For a moment it looked as if Hugh Warren would push past his friend's restraining hand, but he subsided, falling back into his seat. "Yes. You are right, as usual. Since I do not even know where Sarah is sleeping tonight, I would only cause her a scandal pounding on doors to find out." He raised a haggard face to Jack. "But God grant that I can last through the night without knowing that William is safe."

Jack Branton reached out and clasped his friend's shoulder. The look he gave him spoke more than mere words could ever express.

Hugh placed his own hand over that of his friend for an instant, then sighed and let his head fall against the chair's cushioned back to rest.

"Oh, no you don't, sluggard. Up to bed with you," Branton ordered. "And mind you, tell your valet to take great care to make you presentable in the morning. I'll not have you frightening the ladies with that heavy stubble you grow."

His grumbling tone won a reluctant half-smile from his troubled companion.

Arms draped about one another's shoulders, they trailed out of the warm study, through the cold and drafty hall, and stumbled up the broad oak staircase to fall into their respective beds.

Chapter Fourteen

ON HIS WAY TO BEAULIEU THE NEXT MORNING, HUGH pulled his stallion up short when Jervase Warren's gig rushed out through the gates of Althurst into the road and almost ran him down.

"Oh, I say, old man, sorry. Fresh horse and all that."

Triste took advantage of the chance meeting. Taking hold of its bridle, he pulled the fine bay gelding Jervase drove to a complete halt.

Ignoring the gelding's obvious nervousness at the proximity of his stallion, he asked, "Is there any word of William?"

Jervase bristled at the man's audacity. Not only had he taken it upon himself to interfere with *his* horse, but he was asking about *his* cousin by his first name.

His dignity thus twice affronted, Jervase answered testily, "No, there is no word from *His Lordship*," seeking to put the upstart in his place.

He hazarded a wild guess. "And if you are running to ask Sarah if she has seen him, then you are wasting your time. If she had word of him, she would certainly have let me know. *I* am his guardian, after all!"

He frowned mightily. "Why should anyone tell you anything, anyway? No one *knows* you!" With that he blandished his whip ineffectually. "Now let go my horse and get out of my way!"

With a forceful expletive, Hugh spun his horse away from the gig and its useless occupant and galloped away. His mood had not in any way been improved by the encounter with his cousin Jervase. The thought that Sarah might withhold information about William from him infuriated him. Illogically, he felt that she should sense that she could trust him.

At Beaulieu he left his horse standing for the groom who was running from the stables to catch and care for his stallion and leapt up the steps to the door. Of the footman who had come in response to the clatter of a horse's hooves on the paved fore-court he demanded without preamble, "Where is Lady Sarah?"

The footman managed to blurt out, "In the blue drawing room," before being swept aside.

Hugh remembered the room from his visit the other day. Thrusting the door open so hard that it slammed back against the wall, the man called Triste erupted into the drawing room like an explosion.

Sarah dropped the book she was reading and jumped to her feet, shocked eyes wide, her hand pressing her bosom.

"Where is he?" Triste demanded. He crossed the wide room in long, aggressive strides, his face iron-hard. Six feet from her he stopped.

Sarah began to breathe again. Still, it was all she could do to stand her ground in the face of this assault. Never had she been threatened by such a powerful force in all her sheltered young life.

The door opened again and Carsonby entered. His eyes locked on the tense figure of the stranger, he announced in even tones, "I have taken this, my free day, to come see if I may be of service to you, Lady Sarah."

"Get out!" The tall man spun on him, his eyes blazing.

It was more than Sarah could endure. She opened her lips to demand from this *person* how he dare enter her presence so precipitously. How dare he speak to her so! And how *dare* he try to intimidate her servant!

Caution won out over anger as she considered the suppressed rage of the man in front of her, though. Instead of the challenge to his lack of manners that she longed to issue, she ignored him and said with hard-won calm to the butler, "Wine for the gentleman and a cup of tea for me, please, Carsonby."

Carsonby shot her a glance full of his intent to stand by to see to her safety.

Sarah was in command of her emotions now, however. "You may go, Carsonby."

Fairlea's butler backed reluctantly from the room. He touched the doorknob, thought better of it, and left the door to the drawing room standing wide open.

Triste threw a hot glance at the door, then forgot it, growling, "The Viscount. The boy's missing. I've come to hear what you know about it."

"I?" Sarah stalled, offended by his rough manner and by the implication that she might have something to do with William's disappearance. That strengthened her—in spite of the fact that she was guilty. Guilty or not, what right had this man—this stranger—to accuse her!

She raised her chin and looked him in the eye, having made her decision. "What should I know but that he was not at home when I called on him yesterday?"

She was not about to tell this angry man anything that might lead him to William. How could she truly know whether or not he meant the child harm?

Looking at him, she saw a tall, slender man with a harshly handsome face presently ablaze with an intensity that frightened her. His superb body was tense with the strength of the emotions that gripped him, and she was not in any way certain that it was safe to give him the information he demanded.

She lowered her gaze to where his hands hung at his sides. The beautiful, long fingers curled as if they longed to wring the truth from her . . . or as if they longed to wring her neck!

The tension in those hands put Sarah in mind of a bird of prey, all slashing talons. The thought sent shivers down her spine, and strengthened her resolve.

She gave herself a mental shake. To protect William, she must keep her wits about her.

As if he sensed her closing her mind to him, he leapt forward over the last few feet that separated them. Grabbing her by her shoulders, he shook her, hard. "By damn, I will have it from you! Where is my . . . Lord Althurst?"

Sarah tried to keep her voice even in spite of the

shaking. "Unhand me, sirrah!" She said the words with icy disdain.

Her insult penetrated to the man's mind. He dropped her as if she had suddenly burst into flames.

Stepping back, he looked for a moment as if some part of him wanted to apologize. Then his face iced over once more, and his eyes glittered with menace. "The boy. I must find him!"

Sarah was suddenly afraid. Not for herself, but for William. Never would she tell this obviously dangerous man where William was.

She might endanger herself, and, indeed, with the strange power he sometimes exerted over her woman's heart, she had no doubt that one day she would, but William was another matter. She would never entrust *his* safety to an unknown.

Never! At any cost, she would keep the boy's whereabouts safe from this stranger—this man who might be the very source of the danger that threatened the young Viscount.

She sent a prayer for forgiveness winging upward and took a deep, ragged breath for confidence. Then, looking him straight in the eye, she told Triste, "I cannot be of the slightest help to you. I have no idea where Viscount William is to be found."

Quick as a striking snake, he snatched her back to him and peered fiercely down into her eyes. "By God, if I thought you capable of a lie . . ."

He groaned and thrust her from him, sending her staggering back and almost falling into the window seat where she had been reading before he had crashed into the room. Whirling away from her, he charged across the wide expanse of Oriental carpet and out the door.

Sarah sank gratefully onto the cushions of the window seat and stared at the rectangle through which his broad-shouldered form had disappeared. Slowly her scattered wits returned to her.

She put down a sharp pang of guilt. She had told the man a deliberate lie, God forgive her. Even while she hated having had to do so, she could find—search her mind as she might—no alternative.

What else could she have done? He had been raging. And he was a very powerful man.

Absently, she rubbed her arms, where fast-forming bruises attested to his strength. Could she have risked letting him know that William was here, upstairs, safe?

Would William still be safe if she had? Painfully, she admitted that it was not a decision she could risk being in error making.

Until she could force Jack to do some plain talking about this man he had seemed to befriend, Sarah had no choice. As matters stood, she could do nothing but regard Triste as a danger to William.

And no matter how her foolish heart felt about him, there was nothing else she could do. While there existed the possibility that he was William's danger, then Triste would have to be her enemy.

From Sarah at Beaulieu, Triste galloped back to Branton Hall. There, Jack watched the man he knew to be Hugh Warren, Sixth Viscount Althurst, pace the study like a caged beast. Seeing the wild glint in his eyes, he inquired quietly, "What did you learn from Sarah?"

"That she has no idea where William is," he answered shortly, his face reflecting the agony he felt. "My God, Jack. If he has been taken as I was . . . If the slavers are his destination . . ." He turned haunted eyes to his friend. "Young boys . . . It is unspeakable."

He took another rapid turn around the rug in front of the fireplace, pent-up power emanating from him. His anxiety for his younger brother was clearly tearing him apart.

Jack could sense the awful desperation in his friend. He sensed, too, that it would be unwise to waste time falsely reassuring him. "Perhaps they haven't had time to get William out of the country," he said quietly, offering by way of comfort what he hoped might be true.

Althurst jumped at it. "The ports! Of course! I shall go look aboard what ships are in the nearest ports. If he is there, I shall find him!" He started for the door.

Jack couldn't bear to see the raw hope in his face. What if he were sending him on a wild-goose chase? The least he could do was chase with him. "Wait," he called out, "I am coming with you!"

Much later, at Althurst, the danger to William once more came alive. In the deep silence of the middle of the night, it was alert and busy.

Two dark-clad figures crept into the young Viscount's luxurious bedchamber. The smaller of them gestured toward the high bed with its massive carved-oak half-canopy.

Both moved to the side of the bed and stood looking up into it at the deeply carved battle chariots and Roman legions that fought there under the watchful eyes of their gods. So baroque was the carving that the battle it depicted seemed to have movement.

It was the weight of the piece, however, that interested the onlookers, not its artistry. The bull-like taller one grinned. "This should do for 'im when it falls. 'Eavy enough to crush a man full grown, I'd say." He drew a small saw, and something else, from the bosom of his rough coat.

The smaller figure smiled. She held out her hand for the other object he had brought.

"Ere ya' go, sister mine. This 'ere bludgeon 'as flat sides, see? It won't make no round dents where you 'it 'Is little Lordship."

He looked at her intently, to be sure she understood. "When ya' ears this canopy come down"— he pointed to the innocent wooden structure above them—"ya runs in and finishes the job, don't forget."

He drew his hand over the flat surface of the bludgeon almost lovingly. "Because it's flat, it won't leave no marks on 'Is Lordship different from what this 'ere canopy makes." He grinned at her. "And that way there won't be no one the wiser." Tossing both objects on the bed, he rubbed his hands together with satisfaction. Beaming, he waited for his sister's praise.

It was not forthcoming. With a heavy sigh, the man took up the saw and turned to his task.

"Shhh," his sister cautioned. "Have a care you don't make any noise. No one must suspect. And take care that you do not saw through the bolts that hold up the canopy where anyone can see what you've done."

"Do I look like I'm stupid?"

His sister decided the safest course was to give no answer.

For the next few minutes the only sound in the room was the steady keening sound of the saw biting through the thick iron bolts that held the weight of the canopy.

"There!" The man moved back from the bed, satisfied. "When 'Is little Lordship plunks inter 'is beddy-bye . . . smash! "'E'll be squashed like a bug!"

The woman moved closer, as if to see.

"'Ere now! Stay back from it, I sez. I've got it just right. Ya go shoving yer nose in there, and ya just might tumble the lot."

"Very well. I suppose you have done a good job." She threw up her hand to forestall his next comment. "I know, I must be sure I'm the one to turn down his bed tonight. That will be no problem. I have told his maid, Vera, that the Viscount's disappearance has severely overset her and have sent her home to spend a few days with her mother. When the little Viscount turns up, I'll see to it that his bed will be ready for him." She smiled evilly. "Of course the little dear will be exhausted."

Her brother grinned at her admiringly. "Naow, ain't ya the clever one!"

She ignored his compliment and said briskly, "Now let's go back belowstairs before we are discovered. I can easily explain my brother coming to visit me from the stables, but nothing would explain why I had let you up here if we were caught."

At Beaulieu the next morning, William, pretty as a girl with his curls threaded through with a yellow ribbon that exactly matched his gown, was trying to play ball with Fluff without stepping on and ripping the ruffle from his hem.

When Sarah came out onto the terrace, he looked up at her from the lawn and complained, "How do you play ball when you always have to have one hand holding up your skirt?"

"Isn't it maddening?" Sarah grinned at him. At least she was seeing what it would be like if her purpose had been getting revenge on one of the males in her life. "It is simply the way we females must play. Our clothing precludes any other. Now you can see why I prefer riding to any other outdoor pursuit."

William came panting up from the grass. "Huh! But when you go riding you get a constant stitch in your side from sitting crosswise and twisted round on your horse."

Sarah looked surprised. "A stitch?" She cocked her head in thought. "You must be doing something wrong. I do not recall a stitch."

"Aw, you're just so used to it you don't notice it."

"Wilhelmina!" Sarah tried hard not to laugh. "Young ladies certainly do not say 'aw'!"

"Aw, Sarah." William had to tease.

Sarah laughed for him. She was so glad—yes, and relieved—to see that he could attempt to joke with her. Having been through what he had recently experienced—things that no child should ever have to face—William could still laugh.

She was so grateful for this mercy. His innocence had been assailed and sorely tried, but still it lingered. She fervently thanked the Lord.

She rose and walked toward the lawn. "Come. I shall endeavor to play catch with you." She grinned at him over her shoulder. "The trick is to drop your skirt just as you catch the ball, so that you might do it successfully. I'll show you."

William followed her back onto the lawn. Somehow he was not all that enthusiastic about learning to play catch in a skirt.

Chapter Fifteen

❧

THEY STORMED INTO THE SEASIDE TOWN LIKE A WHIRLWIND, four men and eight horses cascading down to the docks in a reckless rush through the narrow cobblestone streets.

Hugh Warren rode at their head, his grim face full of breathless hope. Jack Branton rode close behind him, two pistols stuck in his broad belt, and a look of determination on his face that would give anyone foolish enough to stand in his way second thoughts.

When his friend made a flying dismount and ran toward the gangplank of the first tall ship, Jack caught up his horse and passed the reins to it and to his own to one of the grooms he'd brought along to tend the relief mounts—and for added firepower if needed. Each of them had pistols stuck into their belts too.

Jack had every intention of using the competent men to add to the weight of any argument that might arise when the Sixth Viscount Althurst searched the ships for the Seventh.

The grooms, Simms and Kemp, still smarted under the lash of their own self-recriminations at having failed to keep the young Viscount safe. They were more than eager to serve, no matter what sort of assistance might be needed. They sat their horses at the ready, hoping for a chance to redeem themselves.

That which drove them was nothing, however, to the devils that drove Hugh. Certain that his own long absence had incubated the plot against his younger brother, Hugh was half mad with his determination never to fail to protect the child again.

In his tortured mind he understood that he must now be ever present to stand between William and whatever danger might threaten him! To do less . . . his mind refused even to consider that he might! But to do so he had first to find the boy!

Hugh's spurs rang with the force of his stride as he plunged up the gangway. At the top, a seaman tried to block his passage. "'Ere, naow!"

"Take me to your captain."

The seaman fell back at the sound of that voice. He hesitated only an instant, then turned to lead the way to the captain's cabin.

"Gentl'mun to see ya, Captin." He stood back, feeling he had moved out of the tall man's way just in time to avoid being swept brutally aside.

The captain rose, scowling. "State your business."

"I am looking for my brother. I've come to search your ship."

"The devil you say!"

Jack Branton appeared behind his friend. Shouldering the seaman out of his way, he stepped forward and held out a purse toward the truculent captain. "Choose" was the only word he uttered, but his other hand, resting on the butt of one of the obvious pistols at his midsection, spoke volumes.

The captain fell to cursing under his breath. Hugh spun on his heel and left the cabin. Driven by his terrible anxiety, he began his search of the vessel.

Jack tossed the purse onto the captain's chart table, where it landed with a satisfying clunk. "You are a wise man, Captain. It is a pleasure to recompense you for the small disturbance."

"I ought to stop that fellow."

"It would not have been a good idea to attempt it."

"Why the blazes should I not even now? This is my damned ship!" But something in this second intruder's manner arrested him.

"Captain, my friend will have satisfied himself in a few minutes." He looked the open-faced seafarer straight in the eye. "I propose to you that such a small disturbance is not worth dying to try to prevent."

The captain's brows drew fiercely down, but he remained where he was, silent until Hugh reappeared to tell Jack tersely, "He is not here."

Seeing the anguish on Hugh's face, something he couldn't later explain prompted the captain to say, "You'd better have a care on the next vessel down, damn you. You'll get your heads blown off if you try this sort of thing over there."

Jack dropped his hand from the butt of his gun and jumped forward to seize and shake the startled ship's captain's hand. "Thank you, sir, for your warning. We are sorry to have disturbed you."

Then he was gone, leaping up the ladder to the

deck, and pounding down the gangplank in pursuit of his heedless friend. He caught him at the top of the gangplank of the next ship.

There, two rough men held a snarling Althurst at bay with belaying pins. Althurst tensed to spring, the two seamen crouched to receive his attack, and Jack lunged forward, pistol in hand, yelling, "Stand easy!"

The two men froze into immobility, and Althurst shoved past them to begin his hasty search of their ship. He was down the hatch in a flash.

From where he held the watch at gunpoint on the deck, Branton heard a shout from below. It was followed by the sound of a solid blow and the thud of a heavy body falling.

Belowdecks, Althurst grunted as a fist connected with his body. Taking care in the narrow companionway not to stumble over his first assailant, he proceeded to pound this second, burlier man into unconsciousness.

Seeing the two men lying at his feet made him feel better, somehow. Obviously he had benefitted from the exercise.

Grinning savagely, he kicked open the door they had guarded. Inside, lying bound hand and foot on a filthy bunk, he found a young man. With a kindred feeling ripping at him from his own past, he leapt to the youth's side and tore the gag from his mouth.

As his fingers worked at the knots to free him, the man thanked him profusely. Althurst pulled him from the bunk and set him on his feet, interrupting his spat of gratitude. "I am Althurst. I seek a small boy. Have you seen him? Could he be aboard?"

When the youth could be of no assistance, Althurst pulled him to the ladder and shoved him upward, all interest in the man gone, smothered in his wild need to find his brother.

Turning back, he continued to search the foul-smelling ship. He took infinitely more care than he had spent on the ship under the command of the bluff, honest captain.

Having searched every inch of the vessel, he rushed back to the open deck. He fought devastation at his lack of success.

Jack had hoped the fight he had heard meant that Althurst might have found his brother. When the youth Althurst had freed rushed out on deck, his gag still hanging round his neck, Jack stopped holding his breath.

Greater disappointment followed when, a few minutes later, Althurst reappeared, shaking his head in frustration and sucking a skinned knuckle.

Jack hardly had time to warn the men he held his gun on not to follow before he was forced to run after his friend.

Althurst fared no better at the third ship. He had to make a conscious effort not to let his shoulders sag in defeat by the time he left the fifth.

By the time he had searched every ship in the port, Jack Branton had run out of the money needed to placate and the patience to explain matters to the various captains of the vessels. Wearily the two friends walked back to where Simms and Kemp waited with the horses.

There was no sign of the youth Althurst had rescued. There was very little activity on the docks.

Fog was beginning to swirl around the legs of the horses. Night was approaching.

Jack looked at the strained faces of his grooms, and realized that he, himself, was very near the end of his endurance. One look at Althurst showed him a man driven beyond human reserves by anxiety and the need for action. Still, he didn't know whether he'd be able to call his friend to a halt.

He had failed to take into consideration the awful state of Hugh's mind. When he suggested, "My men are about to drop. The horses need feeding. Indeed, we all could do with a meal," his friend simply let him shepherd him, haggard faced and unresisting, to the inn at the top of the town.

Bespeaking a small private parlor for Hugh and himself, Branton sent his men into the common room with enough coin to buy hearty meals and ale to wash them down. Concerned at Hugh's trance-like compliance with his wishes, he guided him carefully into the parlor, and into the nearest chair.

"My God, Hugh, are you all right?"

Hugh lifted eyes full of agony. "I didn't find him, Jack. I didn't find him."

A hundred replies rose to Branton's lips, but he discarded them all as worthless. Instead he walked over to the door, tore it open, and shouted for the innkeeper's best brandy.

In the dead of the night, as they passed Althurst on their way to Branton, Hugh drew rein. "You go on, Jack. I want to talk to Jervase. I'll be along when I've done so."

Jack opened his mouth to object, then closed it.

He knew better than to think he could dissuade his friend.

Jack and his men rode on to Branton. He kept an eye on Hugh, however, until he disappeared up the long drive to Althurst.

At Althurst, the night porter roused himself at the sound of the knocker. Incredulously, he opened the door.

He almost demanded what the visitor wanted at such an hour, but then he got a look at the man's face. Quick as a flash his need for sleep deserted him and he moved respectfully aside for the man to enter.

When he heard him say, "I have come to speak to Jervase Warren," in a voice such as might have issued from a tomb, no question of raising an objection crossed his mind. With all speed he went to rouse Mr. Jervase Warren.

Hugh waited in the study where he had been told Jervase would join him shortly. He mused that this was the second time he had appeared to announce his identity to someone who believed that he was long dead.

This time, however, he felt no joyful anticipation as he had when he had set out to regain his friend Jack.

This time he had come to make a solemn accusation against the man he suspected was guilty of removing him from his comfortable, ordered life and precipitating him into bitter years of slavery.

This time he had come to do murder if that was what was necessary to discover what had become of his beloved brother, William.

His back was to the door when Jervase entered.

Slowly he turned to face him. He let the silence draw out between them as he stared at the elegant dandy in the long brocade dressing gown.

Finally he spoke. "You still do not know me, then?"

Jervase said peevishly, "Of course I do not *know you*." Jervase attempted to insult his visitor with this inference that he did not recognize him socially. "There is absolutely no one in all *my* acquaintance with the unmitigated gall to arrive at a man's house demanding to be received in the middle of the night!"

"Look more closely. I am told I have greatly changed . . . *cousin*."

Jervase stared, then stared harder. His mouth dropped open. "You aren't . . . You can't be . . . My God!"

The austere night visitor didn't speak. He merely stood silent, a savage smile on his lips.

Chapter Sixteen

JERVASE STOOD FROZEN. HIS HEAD FELT AS IF IT WERE spinning from a blow. Indeed, he felt he had suffered a severe one.

Hugh! Hugh alive after all these years! He stumbled in the direction of the drinks table, mumbling, "You must forgive me. I don't seem to be quite myself." He looked at Hugh a little wildly. "I don't seem to be accepting the evidence of my own eyes."

Slopping a large quantity of brandy into a glass, he raised it to his lips with a hand that shook badly. All but inhaling the glass's contents, he choked and coughed, then focused on his guest.

"Hell's bells, Hugh. What the deuce do you mean showing up here in the middle of the night like this? It's like seeing a ghost. It's enough to give a fellow palpitations of the heart."

Pouring himself more brandy, he threw that down and stared piercingly at his cousin. "Damn it all. It's like being waked up by a blasted intruder!" He looked vaguely at the glass in his hand. "You want some brandy?"

A sharp bark of laughter was his only answer.

Jervase looked at his cousin owlishly. "Well, do you or don't you? Damned if I'm gonna keep after you about it."

Hugh smiled then, certain of his cousin's innocence. He stepped forward to clap his younger cousin on the shoulder. "I'll get it myself, Jerry." He moved to the table and poured himself half a glass of the excellent brandy his father had laid away in his cellars long before the births of the two men drinking it.

"By God that sounds good, Hugh."

Hugh looked over questioningly.

"You were the only one who ever called me Jerry. Always liked that, you know. Made me feel more . . ."—he colored and ducked his head—"manly, somehow."

Hugh merely raised his glass in Jervase's direction and sipped his brandy.

Jervase followed suit, then asked plaintively, "Where have you been, Hugh? And what the devil happened to your nose?"

"My nose was broken in a dispute over my newly acquired . . . *lack* of status after leaving England."

"That sounds damn fishy. Why the deuce did you leave if it meant . . . ? Hell, Hugh. Why did you leave at all? Things have been going in a muddle ever since you left."

Hugh sipped his brandy.

"William got made Viscount after a while, you know. Nice boy, but I can't abide children. The servants told me all was well, and so I stayed in London at first. Then my . . . hmmm, my housekeeper pointed out to me that I was shirking my duty to him. Made me get myself declared his guardian, and I've been moldering away down here in the country ever since."

Hugh frowned thoughtfully.

"Shabby! Shabby of you, Hugh. You should have come back and done your duty. It's been hard going for me in your absence, I can tell you. Hate the country. Hate children. Don't like being here above half!"

Jervase continued his complaint in a lowered voice, "Wouldn't want William to know, but I don't like *him* above half either. Precocious little brat. You'd no business dumping it all on me."

Hugh burst out in startled laughter. "God, Jerry! You can't know the feelings tearing through me! You can't know the relief . . ." Tears filled his eyes, his laugher caught in them.

Jervase closed the space between them. Concern and puzzlement warred in his face. "What is it, Hugh? What's the matter?" He grabbed his cousin's broad shoulders and peered earnestly into his eyes.

Hugh snatched him into a bear hug that threatened to crush him. "Nothing!" he shouted, lifting Jervase from the floor and spinning around with him.

Jervase fought himself free and stood tugging his brocade dressing gown back into neatness. "Good Lord, Hugh! What in the name of all that's holy has come over you?"

Hugh couldn't contain his joyful grin. "You nodcock! I am merely on the border of hysteria to see that you had no knowledge of the tragedy that befell me. The relief has made me giddy, is all."

"Tragedy? What tragedy? I thought all the tragedy happened here at home because *you* slipped away somewhere to write your blasted poetry."

Hugh's laughter died. "Poetry. I had quite forgotten." He looked hard at Jervase. "Did they really think I'd run off to be a poet?"

"No." His cousin blushed. "I just figured that out later for myself."

Hugh's face was serious now. "No, cousin, I did not leave home so that I could indulge my youthful ambition to become a poet."

He regarded Jervase levelly. "I was bludgeoned and dragged into an alley when I went to buy presents for Mother and William. Two months later, I was a slave to an Arab prince."

"I say! That's monstrous!" Jervase displayed typical English outrage.

Hugh smiled tightly. Jervase clearly hadn't been the mind behind his abduction.

He turned his thoughts to the problem. If not Jervase, then who was at the bottom of the plot to clear his way to the title?

Dim as his cousin was, surely he knew that he would be the first to fall under suspicion if both people who stood in his way were removed under odd circumstances? Obviously there was another hand at work here.

Hugh refilled Jervase's glass. "Jerry, when did you decide that William needed you?"

"Huh, I *didn't*. Don't think the little monster needs me yet! He gets along just fine with Sarah Fotheringay and the staff here to look after him. Blasted brat doesn't even appreciate all I gave up for him." He added plaintively, "Doesn't even *like* me, can you believe?"

Hugh let that go without comment and asked instead, "Then why did you come?"

"Oh, well. That's easy. Clara wouldn't let me

have a moment's peace about it. Getting stingy with her affection over it, she was too."

Hugh was very still. "And just who is Clara?"

"Why, Clara is my . . . hmmm, you know, Hugh." Jervase looked embarrassed. "Clara Nethers, my . . . housekeeper."

"I see."

Jervase was relieved that he did. "Thank Heavens! Awkward to explain these things to someone one hasn't seen for ages."

"Send for her."

"You can't be serious!"

Hugh neither moved nor spoke.

Shrugging, Jervase moved to the door and gave the footman outside the study the order to summon the housekeeper.

He returned almost immediately escorting her.

The woman moved into the room confidently. She didn't notice Hugh, who had stepped back into the shadows. "What are you doing, sending for me in the middle of the night, Jervase?"

"Well, it can't be much of an inconvenience, Clara. You're still fully dressed."

"My brother was visiting from the stables. What is it you want?"

Hugh stepped forward. "It is I who desired your presence, Clara Nethers."

She started at his sudden appearance, recovered instantly, and asked uneasily, "And just who might you be, sir?"

"I am Hugh Warren, Sixth Viscount Althurst." He let his voice ring with firmness, using his name and title as a weapon against her.

She quailed. Her face drained of all color and she

swayed on her feet. "It can't be! You can't be! You're dead! He told me—" She cut off whatever she had been about to say, slapping a trembling hand across her mouth.

Hugh moved forward to loom over her. "Who told you?" He reached out and grasped her wrist. Drawing her mercilessly into the candlelight, he demanded, "Speak, woman, who told you I was conveniently dead?"

His grip tightened, and she squirmed, twisting her hand to be free. "Let me go. You're hurting me."

"You have no idea of hurt. The things I have been forced to learn about hurt are beyond your wildest nightmares. You have *yet*"—he breathed the word with soft menace—"to be a slave in Eastern hands, mistress."

She looked into his cold face and her mind manufactured a threat. "No, no! You cannot mean to sell me to the slavers! I never told him to do that! Never!" She was jerking frantically at her own arm, beating at Hugh's hand in a frantic bid for freedom.

His grip never slackened. She read from the dark recesses of her own mind the purpose she imagined she saw in his implacable face. "Nooooo! I only told him to *kill* you! I swear!" She turned to Jervase beseechingly. "I did it for you! I wanted you to be Viscount Althurst!" Her voice became a wail. "I wanted to be a lady!"

Hugh released her then, and she fell in a sobbing heap at his feet.

Hugh looked to where Jervase stood frozen, staring wide-eyed at the complete stranger who had been his mistress for years. Finally he lifted his horrified gaze to Hugh's. "God, Hugh. I didn't know." He shook his head in disbelief. "I didn't know."

Hugh shrugged it away, glad to know that his own blood had not willingly conspired against him. "She has a brother?"

"Yes. An ugly beast of a man. He works in the stables. Grimsby won't have him in the house near the maids." He seemed to be coming out of a trance. "Shall I send for him?"

"If he's the man I remember, better send four strong footmen to bring him."

Jervase headed for the door again. "I'll send six!"

Grimsby was the man outside the door when Jervase opened it. "I was summoned by one of the footmen who says something odd is occurring, Mr. Jervase."

"Right he was!" Jervase gave the order for Nethers to be brought, and the butler nodded his understanding and left to implement it.

Then minutes later, over the muffled sobbing of the housekeeper, they heard the sounds of a scuffle as the men approached the study.

When Nethers was dragged through the door, Hugh shook with a barely governable rage. Here, at last, was the man responsible for his ordeal. As he fought to control himself, Nethers sighted his sister.

"What have ya done?" His face flamed with rage. "Ya bitch!" He lunged toward where she huddled, his eyes blazing murder. "I'll kill ya, ya stupid bitch. If ya told 'em, we'll swing!" Six strong footmen strained to hold him.

The housekeeper rose to her knees and pointed dramatically at her brother. "It was him. I swear it.

He was the one that clubbed you down and sold you to the slavers!"

Grimsby staggered with shock at her words. Then he turned to look at the man she addressed, the color draining from his face. In a voice that broke in joyful recognition he gasped, "Master Hugh?"

Hugh touched Grimsby's shoulder affectionately. "Yes, old man, it is I."

Grimsby turned away to find a task to occupy him before his returned master could see that his joy had unmanned him.

Hugh absently touched the scar on his temple left by the brute's bludgeon. Silently he waited for a feeling of triumph, a surge of satisfaction that he was at last to have his revenge. These two would be hanged for what they had done to him!

He felt nothing. Only weariness. And a sadness for the loss of the years they had stolen from him.

He watched them, one accusing the other and felt only an empty disgust. It was obvious they had no idea where William was hiding. With a gesture, he ordered Grimsby to clear them from the room like the trash he found them.

The danger to William was past. That was the only thing that had significance for him.

As a footman dragged the housekeeper, screeching to a thoroughly embarrassed Jervase of her love for him, out of the room in the wake of her struggling brother, Hugh stood lost in thought. How stupidly futile were all those long years of hatred he had spent. How ridiculous his lovingly nurtured plans for revenge.

Wasted. It had all been a waste of his time. Here

they were, his enemies, the objects of so much passionate thought on his part—two pitiful pieces of human refuse. Neither singly nor together were they worth one moment of the agony of mind he had devoted to them.

He drew a long breath. It was over. The past was gone. He realized now that the only thing worth remembering—the only thing of any value from his long years of captivity—was learning how the remembrance of the loving friendship of little Lady Sarah Fotheringay had enabled him to survive the horror of those years.

He stood for a moment absorbing his new understanding. And there it was. Love was the force that lasted in the end.

Not hate. Not vengeance.

Love. That one word summed up all that he had learned of lasting importance in his years as a slave.

That . . . and gardening.

He threw back his head and laughed.

He saw that the quality of his laughter caused Jervase to flinch away from him, but he could not care about that now.

Now there was only one thing on his mind. William. He *must* find William.

Chapter Seventeen

THE NEXT MORNING AT BREAKFAST, HUGH FRETTED OVER William's whereabouts. The food Jack's butler, Oswood, placed before him remained untouched. The coffee grew cold in his cup.

Jack, aware of the eagerness to find his brother that consumed his friend, suggested, "Let us ride over to Sarah's—wherever the chit is—perhaps she has had word from William."

Immediately Hugh was on his feet. "Yes! That is an excellent idea."

There was such bright hope in Hugh's voice that Jack cringed. All the way to Fairlea he cursed himself for having raised in Hugh what might well prove to be a false expectation.

When the new butler at Fairlea, a sour-faced shadow of the elegant Carsonby, told them, "Lady Sarah has ridden to Bewley to partake of breakfast with her aunt, Lady Penelope," Jack just had to ask, "Where is Carsonby?"

The stiff little man answered, "I believe Mr. Carsonby was instantly discharged when he gave notice of his intent to enter service at Lady Sarah's future establishment."

Jack surprised him by saying "Good!" and they were off, on the way across Fairlea to Beaulieu.

Hugh rode with eager eyes fixed on the way before them. Jack rode with his fingers mentally crossed.

When they arrived at Beaulieu, a groom ran up to take their horses, and Hugh didn't even seem to see the man. He took the front steps four at a time.

Carsonby opened the door for them, but the smile on his face faded when he saw Hugh. Without a word he turned and led them to the small breakfast parlor off the solarium.

Sarah had just finished a respectable breakfast when the two men were ushered in. "Jack," she exclaimed with pleasure. Then, after the slightest hesitation, "Mr. Triste." She acknowledged her second guest with some reserve.

Pen looked up but merely smiled tightly and nodded her greetings. She was uncertain just how to receive Jack, who persisted in being at daggers drawn with her, and she was equally at a loss as to how to welcome Triste, who had stormed so at her niece the last time he had seen her.

Jack saw the way Hugh's eyes fastened on Sarah's face and said, "Penelope, will you walk with me in the garden?"

Pen knew better than to inform him he had forgotten her title or to tell him that the garden was still too damp to walk in. After a glance at Sarah, she rose with only the slightest hesitation, and accompanied him from the room.

When Hugh just stood, his eyes devouring her face as if she were his soul's last hope, Sarah, too, rose gracefully from her place at the breakfast table.

Casting a single glance at the little girl playing in the solarium, she led the way to the drawing room.

There, she hoped the sunlight spilling in through the wide Palladian windows might dispel some of the grimness she felt clung to her visitor.

"Would you like some tea?" Quietly she offered the universal English panacea.

He shook his head, his dark hair falling over his brow at the movement. His eyes reminded her of those of a wounded animal. A mortally wounded animal.

Suddenly she was overwhelmed with the need to comfort this man who had been alternately a threatening stranger and a comforting intimate. Dearest Lord! If only she could have certain knowledge which he was!

Without asking her permission, he sank onto the sofa beside her. He was so close his knee brushed her skirt.

Sarah did not remark, as she ought, on his improper proximity. Instead, she watched him solemnly with sympathetic eyes.

He opened his lips twice as if he would speak, but said not a word. It was as if he would tell her the deepest secrets of his very being with his eyes alone.

Sarah could feel his tension, and took it to herself, as if in sharing it she could somehow ease the intolerable burden she sensed he bore. When he reached for her hands, she yielded them.

He clung to her slender fingers as if they were the only things linking him to reality. "Sarah," he said at last, "last night I went to Jervase and accused him of bringing harm to William. Harm I had failed to prevent."

Sarah would have spoken then, out of the gladness that welled up in her to learn he had wanted to protect William, but he went on. "He sent for his housekeeper. While we awaited her, Jervase admitted that she had been his mistress for years. She is a beautiful woman, ambitious to rise above her station in life. Her ambition was to rise from mistress to countess."

Sarah kept absolutely still. That he should never have spoken to her of such things was of no consequence. She could see that he had something momentous to convey to her, and declined to concern herself with trifles.

Triste went on. "She broke down when faced with the truth of her misdeeds and admitted that she had attempted to clear his way to the title. The idea to dispose of William, she claimed, however, was her brother's.

"Later, when Jervase had the brother brought in, we learned that while he had sawn the timber of the bridge and even told us he had fixed the canopy over William's bed so that it would fall on him the next time William gets into it, it was the woman who poisoned William's milk and who pushed the urn off the roof."

Hugh caressed the backs of Sarah's hands with his thumbs, a gesture to reassure her as she sat watching him, her lovely eyes round, and her soft lips parted in anticipation of his next words.

"To his credit, Jervase was horrified. The woman began to sob and tell him that she had asked her brother to kill the Sixth Viscount so that Jervase could assume control of William and of his estates."

Sarah paled and gasped, half rising. "Hugh! They killed Hugh?" Her eyes filled with tears, and she sank back down.

Hugh fought a desire to cover her trembling lips with his own. Even as his heart soared to see her weep for him, he realized he must rein in his emotions in order to bring her gently to a realization of the truth.

Something that Sarah could only describe as a growl entered his voice as he told her, "It was the brother's idea to sell Hugh Warren to the slavers."

He saw Sarah's face drain of all color as horror warred with hope in her eyes. He went on, his grip on her hands never slackening. "The woman was kindhearted enough merely to wish him dead, she said."

Sarah lifted eyes diamond-bright with the evidence of her regard for Hugh Warren and looked deeply into Triste's eyes. There she saw Hell.

With a little involuntary shudder, she sought to withdraw her hand to reach for a handkerchief with which to wipe away her tears. In the turmoil of her mind, it was as if Hugh and the man beside her were somehow becoming mysteriously entwined. Stunned by the very idea, she listened woodenly as Triste went on.

"Jervase sent six footmen to bring the woman's brother from the stable. Every one of them was needed when he realized what his sister had done. He raged at her like a madman, confessing all."

He looked deep into her eyes and said very slowly, very gently, "Seeing the man's strength"—he paused to give his next words the time he knew Sarah would need with them—"I no longer wondered how I had gotten this." He touched the scar on his temple.

As her mind began to register the meaning of his statement, the day she had first seen that scar came rushing back to Sarah. That day when she had gone to investigate the bridge. Again she sensed the comfort she had felt in his arms, and now she understood!

Sarah's mind spun with the revelation he had just given her.

Her head was awhirl with the emotions that battered her as she listened. Then came—overcoming the wild hope of only a moment ago, the hope that he might know what had happened to her beloved friend, Hugh—the even wilder, blazingly impossible thought that he *was* Hugh Warren. Greatly changed—out of all recognition—but Hugh!

Realization tore through her.

His face swam hazily through her tears. She was powerless in the grip of her emotions to do more than sit and devour with avid eyes that dear face. And very, very gently, certainty filled her heart. Her tears spilled down her cheeks as, at the deepest levels of her being, she recognized and reclaimed Hugh Warren from the dead.

The man beside her slipped to his knees in front of her. His piercing gaze locked with her own tearful one. "Ah, God! Sarah! Remember me, Sarah. Please remember me!"

With a cry from the bottom of her heart, Sarah snatched her hands free and threw her arms around him. Between glad sobs she cried, "Hugh! Oh, Hugh!"

*   *   *

In the garden, Pen walked without speaking beside Jack Branton. Every now and again she threw an assessing glance his way.

Each time, she found him watching her closely. It was both flattering and disconcerting. She was used to being flattered. Being disconcerted was a new experience for her.

Finally she said to him, "You know, I find it rather odd that you have offered such staunch friendship to a complete stranger as suddenly as you seemed to offer it to this Mr. Hassan Triste."

He regarded her seriously from fine brown eyes that held a hint of caution.

She walked on. "You know, I find that you are not *generally* afflicted with the tendency to stutter." She watched him with frank green eyes that held a challenge.

"No," he answered after a long moment. "No, I do not stutter, generally."

"And yet, on several occasions I have heard you stutter when pronouncing the extremely disagreeable first name of your erstwhile new friend."

"Surely you are not saying that Hassan is a disagreeable name." He regarded her evenly across the broad shoulder nearest her.

"I am sure it is quite acceptable where it belongs," she admitted mildly. "Englishmen, however, should be called by English names, no matter how darkened their skins may become after prolonged exposure to the Eastern sun."

"Oh?"

"Indeed."

They walked a while in silence.

"Englishmen should be called John . . ."

He inclined his head as if accepting a fine compliment.

"Or," she continued, "William."

"Yes."

They turned a corner in the path and approached a long arbor that formed a pleasant, shady tunnel. Pen plucked a rose from among those rioting over the arbor. "Englishmen should be called . . . *Hugh—not H-Hassan!*"

She turned toward him and tapped him lightly on the cheek with the blossom, a token punishment for keeping her in the dark about their childhood friend.

Instantly the big man beside her grabbed her wrist and pulled her against him. "Don't tease me, Pen. I have never been one of your London lap-dogs."

She moved back a step rather breathlessly, her hand against his broad chest. "Yes, that is true. You have always been the most difficult man of my acquaintance."

"Is that why you jilted me when Harry Fotheringay came along?"

"I never jilted you! We were never engaged."

"But we were meant for each other, and you knew that, Pen."

Her gaze dropped before his heated regard.

"You knew that." It was a question in spite of the imperative form it took.

"Yes, Jack. I know that."

Jack Branton pulled Penelope Fotheringay into

his arms, and it was as if the years between had
never been.

A joyous cry ringing through the garden. "Pen!
Jack! Where are you? Oh, *where* are you? I have the
most astonishing news! The most, most *wonderful*
news!"

Sarah flew down the steps from the terrace and
across the lawn to meet the complacent couple just
coming out of the arbor. Arriving beside them, she
laughed and cried and told them all at once,
"Hugh! It is Hugh! He is home and safe. Isn't it
wonderful? Oh, isn't God kind?"

Jack merely smiled, acknowledging her bound-
less joy.

Pen hugged her niece and said sincerely, "How
marvelous!"

Then Sarah was off again, dancing on winged
feet to where a quietly smiling Hugh sedately
followed her.

When she reached him, she slid an arm around
his waist and brought him to meet her aunt. "This,"
she announced with shining eyes, "is *Hugh*!"

Seeing Sarah's face, Penelope understood at last
why none of the young men who had courted her
lovely heiress niece had been able to make a dent in
her armor of disinterest. Here before her was the
steel from which that armor had been forged.

Pen smiled and held out her hand. "How do you
do, Hugh." She said it as if she had never seen him
before, and after he had bowed over her dainty
hand, he burst into laughter at the wicked little
knowing look she sent between her niece and him,
the newly returned head of the house of Warren.

"What is it?" Sarah looked from one to the other of the three of them, bewildered. "Whatever are you laughing at?"

As none of them would tell her, but as they all had the good manners to quell their delight, she shrugged and put together the last, desperately sought piece of the puzzle.

"Mina!" She called to the pretty little girl on the far end of the terrace next to the solarium. "Mina, dear, please come and see who has at last come home!"

William hoisted the front of his skirt and came dashing toward them. Beribboned curls bouncing, he skidded to a stop in the midst of them. "What is it, Sarah?"

Pen's throaty laughter answered him, and William turned toward her. "Well, Lady Pen? What's afoot?"

Hugh's eyes devoured the little lady. A smile like those that had caught at Sarah's heart on previous occasions lit his face. "William," he said softly.

"Dash it all!" William turned an accusing face to his older brother. "You have given the game away, sir. I am supposed to be Wilhemina." He frowned at the tall man smiling at him.

Sarah stepped forward and slipped an arm around the boy. "Dear, I have something very important to tell you."

"Yes, Sarah?" He gave her his full attention.

"You don't remember your brother Hugh—"

"Oh, yes I do, Sarah," he interrupted. "You may be sure that Grimsby has kept his memory quite alive for me. I am full of stories about him and I daresay that no more than three days pass—or didn't before I started wearing these disgusting skirts—that I don't stop to look at his portrait." He looked at her earnestly a moment. "Pardon me while I digress, for I must apologize. Please forgive my unpleasant comment. The skirts are not disgusting. It is my disposition that has become disgusting since I began wearing them. They are no end of trouble, and I wonder that you ladies can be as amiable as you are while contending with them. My apologies."

"Oh, William," Sarah burst out, "bother your skirts! I have the most marvelous news for you. Hugh is safe and alive."

William's face lit up. "Truly? Oh, Sarah you wouldn't tease about such a thing. Not you."

Suddenly, he quieted, and without turning his head, slid his gaze toward the tall stranger and locked it there. Finally he turned his head and then his whole body, slowly, as if some part of him might break if he didn't move with the utmost care.

Wide-eyed, he studied the hawklike face. Throughout his perusal, he held his breath. Letting it out with a whoosh, he told them, "The eyes. The eyes are the same as in the portrait."

He reached out to his brother, and embarrassed himself by bursting into tears. Swept into a bear hug of an embrace, he threw his arms around his older brother's neck as if he would never let go. "Oh, Hugh! How very glad I am that you have come home!"

Pen and Jack put their arms around a quietly sobbing Sarah and led her away toward the house.

The three of them understood that this moment was too precious for the brothers to share.

William looked hungrily into his miraculously resurrected brother's face. He felt his embarrassment fade as he saw his own tears echoed in those of his long-lost brother.

Chapter Eighteen

Now that she was residing at Beaulieu, Sarah had no need to rely on Letticia for news of the neighborhood social affairs. She was flooded with invitations in her own right. It was with a tremendous excitement that she read and reread her announcement of this night's Assembly.

Hugh would, of course, attend.

She missed him so dreadfully. He had come back from the dead, only to disappear into the morass of legal complications created by his resurrection.

Yesterday, she had received word by messenger from London that he would be home today. He had begged her to see him and promised he would seek her out wherever she might be.

His letter, already perused a hundred times since its arrival, lay safely in her jewel box. To her, it was the most precious thing the box contained.

She could hardly believe how slowly the hands circled the face of every clock she consulted throughout the long day. Since she had just this morning sent a note to Althurst to await Hugh's arrival telling him she would meet him at the Assembly tonight, time had all but slowed to a halt.

While enduring the endless waiting, Sarah alternately soared to heights of hope and plummeted to depths of doubt. Suppose Hugh thought of her merely as the child he had comforted? Merely as a dear friend. Would she survive that?

She had no idea how, or when she had done so, but she had somehow transferred her childish adoration for a comforting young friend to a woman's love for the man he had grown to be. She groaned softly as fears that he might never reciprocate assailed her.

Pen breezed into the room. "What in the world was that dismal sound, my pet?" She moved to the bed where Sarah had tumbled every gown that might have been suitable to wear to the Assembly ball. "Are you in such agony over what to wear tonight?"

Sarah fought the urge to burst into tears.

Pen relented. Going to her niece, she gave her a hug. "You are going to have a splendid time tonight, dear. Stop fretting."

She took up a brush from Sarah's dressing table and put the girl's dusky curls—pulled apart as she tormented herself over Hugh—back into order. "You shall wear your new blue gown, and you shall look so beautiful that no man will be able to resist you."

"Oh, Pen. Why do I feel so pulled in all directions? Why am I so glad one instant and so melancholy the next?"

Pen looked at her solemnly. "My dear . . ."—she let a little time pass as she searched the earnest young face—"you are in love."

Sarah whirled away from her and would have thrown herself on the bed to weep, but it was piled high with her gowns. She stood in the middle of the floor and wailed instead. "Oh, Pen. I know I am in love, but why does it have to be so miserable!"

Pen took her by the hand and led her to the love seat in front of the balcony's open French doors. Pushing her niece down gently, she told her, "You are miserable because you do not realize that he returns your affection."

Sarah fought not to sob. She said in a tight little despairing voice, "No, I am quite certain he returns my affection. Hugh and I were always close." She raised timid eyes to her aunt. "I fear that he might not return . . . my *love*."

Pen resisted her strong inclination to tell her she had seen Hugh's face the other day when the four of them stood in the garden and was certain Sarah's fears were groundless. She said instead, "Where is my Sarah?"

Sarah looked startled. "What do you mean?"

"Well, my dear, *my* Sarah is a strong-minded young lady who gallops about the countryside protecting imperiled young Viscounts, demanding assistance of her neighbors to uncover villains, and investigating suspicious happenings. This beautiful young lady before me is a quaking jelly of a girl, and I want to know where *my* Sarah has gone."

Sarah laughed then. She could feel her old spirit return. "You are quite right, Aunt. Your Sarah's wits, at least, had gone begging. Thank you."

She smiled tremulously. "If Hugh Warren doesn't love me now, I shall just have to go about making him do so shortly, shall I not?"

"That's my girl!" Pen jumped up and headed for

the bed. Now Sarah would be able to choose a gown!

She didn't want to dispel the mood of confidence she had called forth in her niece, so she deliberately neglected to tell her that she had not a thing to worry about. Unless, of course, being dragged to the altar and forced to become a Viscountess ranked among Sarah's fears. Somehow Penelope thought not.

When Penelope turned from the mass of expensive finery on the bed, she found her Sarah indeed had returned. The eyes regarding her were speculative.

"Since you think it a fine thing that I investigate, Pen, surely you will not mind helping me."

Pen braced herself. "Of course not, dear." She didn't meet her niece's gaze, however.

"It comes to me that you have known Jack before."

"Hmmm," Pen assented vaguely.

Sarah all but exploded. "Why did you not tell me?"

"Oh, Sarah. It was so long ago. You were a baby when Jack and I were in love"—she ignored Sarah's open mouthed astonishment—"and you were a mere toddler when your uncle came and laid siege to my heart." Her tone was rueful.

Sarah was incredulous. "How *could* you have preferred Uncle Harry to Jack?"

"I was flattered and swept off my feet." Her face was more serious than Sarah had ever seen it. Very softly she said, "Believe me, I was not long in realizing that I had mistaken my heart. And I have had long years to repent of it."

"And now?" Sarah felt as if she had been holding her breath for minutes.

Pen's smile was as radiant as it was full of secretive promise. "Now, my prying little favorite niece, it is time for us to dress for the assembly ball!"

The night air was soft with the warmth of August and scented with the fragrance of the honeysuckle that ran riot in the hedges surrounding the Little Fairview Assembly Hall. Sarah wore a soft smile of anticipation and her excitement mounted as they approached the hall.

Pen was certain Sarah had never looked lovelier. When they stepped down from the carriage, Sarah was, as usual, instantly surrounded by her friends. Pen had eyes only for Jack Branton, who moved forward to claim her before she had even reached the entry.

Smiling, each greeted the other with eyes that spoke volumes. Without a word they went inside with the laughing crowd.

Sarah pretended she had nothing more on her mind than to laugh and chatter with her lifelong friends, but her gaze flew around the room. Hugh had not come! Her spirits plummeted.

Sternly she told herself, *Hugh has not come yet*, and felt her spirits rise. What an unbalancing effect this being in love was having. She hoped there was a way of overcoming the tendency her emotions had to seesaw.

Then there was a commotion at the door. Turning toward it like a compass needle seeking North, Sarah saw him arrive.

Tall and elegant in his evening black, he stood among a crowd of men. Broad-shouldered, he towered above them all. Dark head bent, face softened by his wonderful smile, he accepted the well-wishings of all his neighbors and friends.

Sarah thought her heart would tear loose from her breast and fly to him. If anyone had happened to be looking her way, they would have seen the blazing light of her love for him making her face radiant.

And then, as if drawn by a force too powerful to resist, he looked up. And in that instant, Sarah was filled with the soaring confidence of a woman for whose man no other woman existed.

For one instant their eyes locked, conveying the depths of their feelings, pledging their souls, promising untold joy.

Then someone slapped him on the back, claiming his attention, and Sarah turned away so that he might bestow it on his friend.

Her own friends occupied her then, chattering excitedly about the handsome Viscount who had had such adventures and had returned just in time to save his younger brother from unspeakable villains. Sarah seemed to listen to them all, but in reality she heard only the song in her heart.

When the orchestra, brought down from London for the assembly, as was the custom in Little Fairview, struck up, several of the young men of their set came to bespeak dances with Sarah. Unable to help herself, she glanced toward Hugh.

Still held by well-meaning friends eager to welcome him home again, he could only frown at the sight of the men around Sarah. Sarah's heart lilted to see his frown, and the smile she bestowed on the young man who led her into the first dance all but destroyed his ability to remember the steps.

When finally Hugh could come to her, the ball was half over. He cut his way through the crowded room to her side with his gaze fixed firmly on her face.

As he went, there were sighs and titters from the ladies as they recognized the purpose with which he approached their friend Sarah. On several faces there were looks of envy.

Sarah was unaware of them all. Her complete being was centered on the man who came to her side and swept her out onto the small balcony behind her.

Neither of them registered the murmur of conversation that arose at their departure.

"Sarah!"

She smiled and said softly, "Good evening, Hugh."

"I thought I would never be free to come to you." His brows drew down in a frown. "Who was that man with whom you danced first?"

Sarah laughed with delight, understanding instantly. "The dance was his." She reached up to touch his cheek, and told him softly, "But the smile belonged to you."

He caught her hand where it touched his cheek, turned his head and kissed her palm.

Sarah drew a sharp breath.

Hugh smiled a wicked smile. "Does that touch you, Sarah?"

She said in a voice that was not quite steady, "I am sure that was not proper." Before he could take her words as a rebuke she added, "Because it made *me* feel most *im*proper."

"Ah, Sarah." He threw a quick glance behind him, saw Jack's broad shoulders and Pen's lovely, slender back as their friends stood shield for their privacy, and reached out for her.

Sarah met him halfway.

Epilogue

THEY STOOD ON THE BALCONY OF SARAH'S ROOM AT Althurst and looked out over the moonlight-silvered surface of the lake.

Leaning back against his broad chest, she sighed. "Happy?"

"Beyond words."

They stood a moment more, then he turned her in his arms so that he looked down into her face. "I love you, Sarah."

She smiled. The light in her eyes told him she loved him, too, with all her heart.

"I love you because you are brave and true. Because you are selfless and dear." He drew her closer and rested his cheek on her curls. "I love you because of the loving friendship we shared and the way it sustained me in my captivity when its memory was all I knew of the kindness that had once existed in the world."

Sarah stirred and would have pulled away to look at him, but he held her fast and she subsided.

Hugh went on. "I love you for hoping against hope that I would return. For praying for my safety instead of my eternal rest."

Sarah squirmed free at that. "How did you know?"

He chuckled and she felt the rumble of it in his chest against the palms of her hands. "My last birthday I heard you speak to your mare."

"You were at your grave!"

"Luckily not in it."

Sarah pressed close again, hugging him fiercely to her.

After a moment he began again. "I love you for putting flowers on my grave . . . and for not minding my scars."

She whimpered at that, and he lightened his tone. "And I love you for keeping that young pest of a brother of mine safe. Though I do *not* like the way you placed yourself in jeopardy at the bridge in your efforts to do so."

Struggling to recover from the pain his mention of the scars from his captivity had brought her, she forced herself to ask lightly, "To which time at the bridge do you refer?"

"The first time, when you almost fell from your horse and might have drowned!"

She looked up at him. "How very odd."

"What is odd?"

"I felt very much more in danger the second time." There was a hint of laughter in her voice.

He stood very still. "Before I pursue that, let me finish what I have begun." He smiled down at her. "A gift to commemorate the gift of your love."

He reached for her hand and held it in his own, palm upward. With his other hand he reached into the pocket of his dressing gown.

Shining in the soft moonlight, the luminous string of pearls that had been her grandmother's gift and

that she had sold to save his brother slipped down
into her waiting hand.

Tears sprang to her eyes, only to be kissed away.

"Now tell me why you felt much more in danger
the second time at the bridge."

She dropped her gaze. "Because that was the
time you . . ."—she faltered at the light that began
to burn in his eyes—"held me in your arms."

"Like this?" he breathed, and suddenly, master-
fully, he swept her up to lie against his chest.

Sarah's eyes were alight with love.

His lips found hers as he turned his back on the
enchanted view of the moon-silvered lake and
carried her into the room.

*If you enjoyed this book,
take advantage
of this special offer.
Subscribe now and get a*

FREE
Historical
Romance

No Obligation (a $4.50 value)

Each month the editors of True Value select the four *very best* novels from America's leading publishers of romantic fiction. Preview them in your home *Free* for 10 days. With the first four books you receive, we'll send you a FREE book as our introductory gift. No Obligation!

If for any reason you decide not to keep them, just return them and owe nothing. If you like them as much as we think you will, you'll pay just $4.00 each and save at *least* $.50 each off the cover price. (Your savings are *guaranteed* to be at least $2.00 each month.) There is NO postage and handling – or other hidden charges. There are no minimum number of books to buy and you may cancel at any time.

Send in
the Coupon
Below

To get your FREE historical romance fill out the coupon below and mail it today. As soon as we receive it we'll send you your FREE Book along with your first month's selections.

Mail To: **True Value Home Subscription Services, Inc., P.O. Box 5235
120 Brighton Road, Clifton, New Jersey 07015-5235**

YES! I want to start previewing the very best historical romances being published today. Send me my FREE book along with the first month's selections. I understand that I may look them over FREE for 10 days. If I'm not absolutely delighted I may return them and owe nothing. Otherwise I will pay the low price of just $4.00 each: a total $16.00 (at least an $18.00 value) and save at least $2.00. Then each month I will receive four brand new novels to preview as soon as they are published for the same low price. I can always return a shipment and I may cancel this subscription at any time with no obligation to buy even a single book. In any event the FREE book is mine to keep regardless.

Name

Street Address   Apt. No.

City   State   Zip

Telephone

Signature
(if under 18 parent or guardian must sign)

Terms and prices subject to change. Orders subject to acceptance by True Value Home Subscription Services, Inc.

11550-9